I0568086

SOUL
TRADER

CHRIS NIBLOCK

Copyright © Chris Niblock 2013

The right of Christopher Niblock to be
Identified as the author of the work has been
Asserted by him in Accordance with the Copyright,
Designs And Patents Act 1988.

All rights reserved.
Apart from any use permitted under UK
Copyright law, no part of this publication may be
Reproduced, stored in a retrieval system, or
Transmitted, in any form or by any means, without
The prior written permission of the publisher.

All characters in this publication are fictitious
And any resemblance to real persons, living or
Dead, is purely coincidental.

ISBN 978-0-9572442-7-6

Published by Focalpoint
5 Vernon House, Watling Street South
Church Stretton SY6 7BG

DEDICATION

For Derek and Colum: fellow sinners and members of the Tuesday Night Club.

By the same Author

Back Dated

CONTENTS

GAMES PEOPLE PLAY
Two Short Stories

CHRIS NIBLOCK

ACKNOWLEDGEMENTS

Thanks to Lesley Douglas for her invaluable assistance in proofreading the text. Any errors and omissions that remain are mine and mine alone.

CHRIS NIBLOCK

"Hell is just a frame of mind."
Christopher Marlowe – *Dr. Faustus*

"For what profit it a man, if he shall gain the whole world,
And lose his own soul?
Mark VIII – *King James Bible*

"We are each our own devil, and we make this world our hell."
Oscar Wilde

Somehow our devils are never quite what we expect when we
meet them face to face.
Nelson DeMille

"Hell is other people."
Jean-Paul Sartre

CHRIS NIBLOCK

Part One

Temptation

CHRIS NIBLOCK

1: SIGN YOUR NAME AND CROSS YOUR HEART

Owen Leadbeater pulls the ring on a can of lager and takes a large swig of the cold, gassy liquid. He has been drinking steadily since lunchtime and so far has consumed the equivalent of nine pints. The reason for this booze-fest is standing on the mantelpiece; a solitary birthday card with the number 40 emblazoned on the front in large, embossed silver numerals. He raises his beer can as if about to propose a toast, then, swinging his arm back, angrily hurls it at the card, knocking it off the shelf and spraying beer all over the chimney breast. The can clatters onto the tiled hearth where it continues to glug out what's left of its contents.

'You can beam me up now,' he yells, throwing his head back and his arms up as if expecting someone to lower a rope and haul him skyward. 'I've had enough, more than enough. My fortieth birthday, the big four oh, and all I get is one lousy card from a brother I haven't seen in years!'

Owen doesn't blame his brother for this lack of contact so much as that stuck up wife of his - Patricia. Patricia, mind you, not Pat or Tricia; she is very particular about that. In fact, she is very particular about everything and like Mrs Danvers in Rebecca she keeps their large detached house as if it were a shrine to the god of *Homes and Gardens*. You didn't visit with his brother and his wife so much as view a show home. One was permitted to look, but on no account to touch the beautiful, and by definition, expensive items on display there. On the rare occasions he has been allowed to enter this palace of middle-class virtue, Owen has at times found himself holding his breath, fearful that in breathing out he might dull the shine on the highly polished mahogany dining table – Waring and Gillow – a snip at two thousand pounds.

'More money than sense, if you ask me,' he bellows drunkenly. Not that anybody is asking, he reflects with some bitterness. 'Some party, eh?' He waves an invisible tankard at the empty room. 'Happy birthday, Owen. Here's to forty years of being pissed-on from a great height.'

Swaying like a sailor on the deck of a storm-tossed ship, Owen navigates an erratic path to the kitchen where, after several fumbled attempts, he manages to yank open the fridge door and grab another can of lager. Returning to the living room in the same ziz-zag fashion, he pulls the ring and with beery foam fizzing over his fingers, raises the can high in the air.

'Come on then God, if you do exist, come and get me. I'm offering you my soul on a plate. It's on special offer this week.' He quaffs some more beer before continuing. 'Well, what are you waiting for? I've been a good boy. That was the deal, wasn't it? Be a good boy all your life and you'll go to heaven. Well? I stuck to my side of the bargain. I've been legal, decent and honest; always kept my nose clean.' His eyes begin to fill with tears and he wipes them away with the back of his hand. 'And look where it's got me – one lousy birthday card.' He checks himself. 'No, I tell a lie; just a small stain on an otherwise unblemished life, believe me. I did have one other card, but it doesn't count. It doesn't say 'happy birthday', it just has a picture of a bowl of fruit on the front – you know, a still-life, and on the back it says, 'this card is left blank for your own message.' From my ex, that one; didn't even put best wishes, just to Owen from Maureen. We were married for the best part of fifteen years and she can't even bring herself to write happy fucking birthday. Blank for your own message, but you're not supposed to leave it blank are you!' he shouts, snot mingling with the tears he can no longer control.

In something approaching an out of body experience, Owen looks down on the pathetic wretch that he has become; sees a grown man who has fallen to his knees and is howling like a baby. He pities, and at the same time, despises this tragic figure but is powerless to help him. A floodgate has opened up, and years of suppressed emotions, bitterness and disappointment are suddenly released; a tsunami that is totally overwhelming and unstoppable.

Fifteen years... that ought to count for something, he reflects, once the emotional tidal wave that has engulfed him recedes a little and he can breathe normally once more. After all, forty is a milestone in any man's life. The least she could have done was to wish him a happy birthday. A blank card, an empty space – it was a perfect metaphor for their married life, one which they hadn't even managed to fill with children.

The wretch on his knees raises his face heavenwards. 'Love… that's your big thing isn't it? Your great gift to the world? I missed out on that one actually. I don't know if you noticed. Did you hear me? I said, I missed… hello, is there anybody there? No? Well, perhaps there's a hotline I can ring. Get them to put a call out, come in number 52, your time is up. Sorry it wasn't much of a life, but there you go. Luck of the draw I'm afraid. Better luck next time, old chap. Oh, sorry, I forgot. There is no next time!'

On hands and knees Owen crawls over to a shabby armchair and hauls himself up onto the seat. No easy task for a drunken man, further handicapped by the can of lager he insists on taking with him on this arduous journey. When he raises the can to his lips he is surprised to find that it's half empty and his shirt front is sodden.

Oh what the hell, he muses. God probably doesn't exist anyway. It was all down to the big bang; nothing one minute – a vacuum – then, KABOOM, you have an expanding universe. Life was nothing more than a series of random events and accidents. You could sum it up in one word – chaos. There was no guiding hand, no omnipotent creator. You might just as well throw a dice as try and plan your life. Still, it was worth one more try.

'OK, I'm going to give you one last chance,' he says out loud. 'It's a once in a lifetime opportunity I'm offering you here. Are you going to take it or not? You haven't got the monopoly on the afterlife you know. I can take my soul elsewhere. There's always the other lot. I just felt I ought to give you first refusal, as it were. So, if you could just give me a sign; one knock for yes, two for no or something... anything?'

In the silence that follows, Owen becomes acutely aware of the everyday ambient sounds of the house that would barely register with him at any other time; the soft ticking of the carriage clock on the mantelpiece; the occasional burp from the hot water tank in the airing cupboard on the landing upstairs, but of divine intervention there is no sign or sound.

'That's a no, then? Okay, Hell it is. I'll get a warm welcome there, if nothing else.' Arching his back, Owen thrusts his free hand down the back pocket of his jeans. It's a difficult balancing act for an inebriated man, and he struggles to extract the object he is seeking. So much so, that by the time he lowers himself back into his chair, Owen is red-faced and breathing hard. The hand resting in his lap cradles an amber-tinted, Perspex tube of tablets. Small and white, they nestle together like the incubating larvae of a malevolent insect. Through narrowed eyes, he studies the label intently for a time then, as if coming to a sudden decision, he removes the plastic stopper with a flick of his thumb. Raising the tube to his lips, he tips some of the pills into his mouth. They taste bitter on his tongue, but he continues to hold them there a moment longer before taking a hurried swig of beer, and swallowing them down. Tears striping his face, he repeats the process until the tube is empty and, feeling very sleepy now, curls up in the armchair like a contented cat. Within minutes he is snoring noisily, an empty beer can still cradled in his lap.

*

It's eight o'clock in the morning and brilliant sunshine is blazing through the un-curtained windows when Owen rouses from his sleep. As he uncurls his cramped limbs from the confines of his narrow armchair, he is surprised to discover that he is not alone in the room. Standing between him and the window and haloed by the blaze of light behind him is a tall, smartly dressed young man with a face that belongs in a Renaissance painting; a man so strikingly handsome that beautiful is not too strong a word to use to describe him. For some moments, Owen believes that God has taken him up on his offer of the night before and he is in the presence of an angel; perhaps the Archangel Gabriel himself.

This supernatural being is carrying a leather briefcase and Owen wonders if this contains a ledger in which the transgressions of his misspent life are recorded and on which he is about to be judged. He also wonders why, if he is in heaven, he is apparently still sitting in his own lounge with its faded carpet and tired looking furnishings. Or is this just an illusion; a stage set; a way of lessening the sudden shock of discovering you have died by providing you with familiar surroundings until you get used to the idea of no longer being alive.

A driver honking his horn in the street outside and a neighbour shouting abuse back at him breaks the spell, and Owen realises with a start that he is not in fact dead, just suffering from an almighty hangover. Leaping from his chair, he scurries round behind it.

'What the fuck! Who the hell are you and what are you doing in my house?'

'You sent for me, I believe,' replies the young man in a soft, slightly effeminate voice that matches his androgynous looks.

'I did? When?' Owen enquires, wonders if this unexpected visitation is the result of a drunken call to a random number he came up with himself or one he plucked from the telephone directory.

'Yesterday evening.' His visitor flips open the briefcase and, withdrawing a manila file, consults it. 'Let me see… ah yes, here we are. Call received at eleven thirty-two and ten seconds precisely. Ring any bells?'

'That's impressively precise, but the only bell ringing round here last night was my front door bell. Just about everyone I know was here helping me celebrate my fortieth birthday,' he lies. 'Place was heaving.' It suddenly occurs to Owen that his visitor hadn't rung the bell. 'How did you get in, by the way? You shouldn't creep up on people like that, scared the life out of me, waking up to find you standing there.'

'Sorry about that but there's no need for concern on that score, you're not due to pass over until three months after your seventy-fifth birthday; June the twenty-first, two thousand and fifty-seven, to be precise.'

Owen can't help laughing at this prediction but his laughter is tempered with a degree of nervousness. His visitor has a certain stage presence; an undeniable gravitas that is both unsettling and totally convincing. A consummate actor or an outright fraud he may be, but Owen is inclined to believe him.

'Who are you?' he asks in an awe filled voice.

The young man approaches Owen's chair and, like a conjuror performing a card trick, produces a business card with a flick of the wrist, 'My card, sir.'

Owen reaches over the back of the armchair and takes it from him. 'Sebastian Tantalus, unusual name but I've never heard of you. You sure you've got the right Leadbeater, only there are several in the book.'

'Book?'

'The phone book.' There is no address or phone number on the front of the card; just Sebastian's name and below it the words 'Carpe Dium' which Owen assumes must be the name of the company the man works for. He turns the card over and, finding the reverse is blank, turns it back again. 'Your number in there is it, or are you ex-directory?'

Sebastian flashes a mouthful of white teeth as brilliant as diamonds. 'Oh, I think you could say we're strictly… ex-directory.'

'So, how did I get your number?'

'How do you mean?'

'I phoned you, you said. If you're not in the book – how did I get your number?'

Another dazzling flash of those perfect teeth. 'Ah, with you now, I didn't say you phoned. I said you called.'

Owen is growing tired of this verbal ping-pong. He has a blinding head-ache and his blood sugar level is dangerously low. If he doesn't get some caffeine and a couple of paracetamols inside him and soon, his head is going to explode 'Called… phoned. What's the bloody difference?'

His visitor by contrast remains maddeningly calm. 'Cried out in your extremis? You know, appealed to a higher court?'

Owen steps out from behind the armchair and

thrusts the card back into his visitor's hand. 'Look, I'm sorry; I'm having trouble following this. It's probably the hangover or maybe I'm still asleep and this is some weird, alcohol induced dream, but just what the fuck are you on about?'

Sebastian places a slim hand on Owen's shoulder. 'I've come for your soul, old love.'

Owen's jaw drops. 'My soul... so, I was right, you are an Angel.'

'It's sweet of you to say so, but sadly no, I'm batting for the other team, as it were.'

'That doesn't surprise me,' murmurs Owen under his breath.

Seemingly oblivious of this aside, Sebastian continues in a whisper, 'you know... *the fire and brimstone brigade.* I'm what you might call a fallen angel.'

Suddenly Owen doesn't feel too well; there's a buzzing in his ears and he feels decidedly nauseous. When he wipes a hand across his forehead, the skin feels cold and clammy. He staggers and has to grip the back of the chair with both hands to prevent himself from falling. Taking hold of his arm in a surprisingly strong grip for such a slim man, Sebastian guides Owen around the chair and lowers him into it, where he sits slumped forward with his head cradled in his hands.

'Oh God, the doctor warned me if I didn't stop drinking something like this would happen; blackouts, memory lapses – hallucinations,' he moans.

His visitor gives a theatrical cough. 'Excuse me, but I am still here you know. I'm not a figment of your imagination. I am, therefore I exist, to quote one of our more eminent residents.'

Owen's head jerks up. 'Really, Neil Diamond is in hell?'

Sebastian arches an eyebrow 'Neil who?' he queries.

'It's OK, forget it. I'm talking rubbish. Neil's not dead. And anyway he said, *"I am, I said"* – not the other thing.'

Sebastian considers this for a moment. 'I am, I said – what's it supposed to mean?'

'It sounds better when you sing it,' Owen assures him.

Sebastian is about to launch into song but Owen forestalls him. 'Please don't. My head feels as though it's about to explode, and I can't believe I'm explaining Neil Diamond's lyrics to one of Beelzebub's little helpers.' He collapses back into the chair.' Oh God, what have I done?'

'Cheer up. It's not that bad. We won't collect until you're seventy-five, as long as you don't breach your contract.'

Owen shoots back up again. 'Contract... what contract?'

His visitor delves into his briefcase and with a flourish, produces a document. 'Ta da! Here's one I prepared earlier,' he declares. 'It's all quite straightforward really. I'll just whizz through the main points. I, Owen Leadbeater, that's you of course, hereinafter known as the party of the first part, do hereby solemnly agree to surrender my immortal soul to His Satanic Majesty, hereinafter known as the party of the second part, on expiry of this contract, or before on demand, should I be in breach of any of the clauses set out in the attached schedules.' Sebastian dismisses these with a wave of his hand. 'There's rather a lot of those so I think we'll just cut to the chase, as they say. It's a standard contract. No special clauses. In return, the party of the second part agrees to use his considerable powers to enable and assist the party of the first part to achieve all his earthly desires. Not bad, eh?'

Sebastian stands there beaming like the Cheshire cat, as though he has just performed an amazing conjuring trick, but there is no applause from his audience of one.

'This *is* what you wanted?' says Sebastian, his irritation at Owen's lack of enthusiasm evident in the sharper tone in his voice.

'Yes and no. I mean, it's a big commitment. This isn't some piddling life insurance policy you're asking me to sign.'

'But don't you see, that's exactly what this is.' He flourishes the document, bringing it down with a smack on the palm of his free hand to emphasise each point. 'A seventy-five year life span – *smack* – guaranteed. A successful, a spectacularly successful if you wish, career of your choice – *smack* – guaranteed. Whatever you want, whatever you need – *smack* – it's guaranteed. G-U-A-R-A-N-T-E-E-D!' Sebastian gives a contemptuous laugh, 'And still he hesitates. Time you woke up and smelt the coffee, my friend.'

At the mention of coffee Owen's eyes light up. 'Coffee... now you're talking. I would kill for a cup of coffee right now. My head's hurting so much, I can't think straight.'

'Owen, when I said, wake up and smell the coffee, I was of course speaking metaphorically.' Owen mimes lifting a cup to his lips. 'You're expecting *me* to make you a coffee?' his visitor asks incredulously.

17

'Yes. I wouldn't have thought that would be too difficult a task for a man who's offering to hand me the world on a plate.'

Sebastian's eyes narrow and his eyebrows come together to form a dark 'V'. The finely sculpted features take on an altogether uglier twist, and Owen fears he may have pushed this dark angel too far. Owen flinches as Sebastian tosses the contract into the air, and then brings his hands together with a sharp slap. When he opens them again, he holds the contract in one hand, and a Costa take-away carton of coffee in the other. With due ceremony, he hands the hot beverage to a visibly stunned Owen, then proceeds to give him a smart tap on the head with the rolled up contract.

'A small demonstration of the powers at my disposal my friend, I assure you,' he says with just a hint of venom in his tone.

Anxious to avoid making matters worse by saying the wrong thing, Owen elects to remain silent; concentrates instead on carefully removing the lid from his carton of coffee and, aware of the irony involved, breathes in the strong, dark aroma of arabica beans. The coffee, when he takes a tentative sip, is surprisingly hot and Owen wonders how Sebastian pulled off this seemingly impossible trick – if indeed it was one – without scalding himself in the process. His natural timidity, and a terror of the horrors his visitor could inflict upon him if he is what he claims to be, however, deters him from seeking an explanation.

As he quietly sips his coffee, Owen uses the time to study his charismatic visitor more closely. Sebastian's good looks aren't restricted to his finely chiselled face, he is also extremely well-dressed in an exquisitely cut charcoal grey suit that could only have been tailored in Savile Row. The pale pink shirt too looks bespoke, as do the black leather Oxford shoes. It is clear, even to an unsophisticated shopper like Owen, who buys most of his clothes from his local supermarket, that no expense has been spared in putting this impressive ensemble together. All six foot of him, from the top of his swept back, black hair down to the toes of his highly polished, black shoes, bears the stamp of quality and good taste. The shoes alone would have cost Owen the best part of a month's wages in the days before he was made redundant 18 months ago. A bit of a dandy is our Mister Sebastian, Owen decides, but is still not sure if he is the fallen angel he claims to be, or just a clever conjuror. The pride the man takes in his appearance, his vanity seem all too human and yet there is something about him – Owen couldn't yet say what – that points to the unearthly.

Owen drains the last of his coffee but playing for time, continues to take the occasional sip from the empty carton. Sebastian's dark eyes narrow to slits and with a shudder, Owen realises that he has been rumbled. It's uncanny, as though the man can read his mind, or has x-ray vision.

'Now that you've had your caffeine fix perhaps we can get back to the business in hand,' he says sharply. Producing a pen, seemingly from thin air, Sebastian hands it and the contract to Owen. 'Just complete the declaration and sign here,' he adds, pointing to the relevant section at the foot of the document.

'A ball point?' queries Owen, pen poised in his hand. 'Shouldn't it be in blood?

'Much too melodramatic darling, plain old-fashioned ink is

perfectly acceptable and just as legally binding, you'll find.'

Just as well, thinks Owen, as he turns his attention to the list, he can't stand the sight of blood.

I the undersigned do hereby swear that I have committed each of the following deadly sins. (Please tick appropriate box)

Lust

Gluttony

Greed

Sloth

Wrath

Envy

Pride

Chewing nervously on the end of the pen, he proceeds to re-read it several times more.

Sebastian, meanwhile, is displaying increasing signs of irritation; retrieving his briefcase, he paces the floor, dramatically shooting his cuff and consulting his watch at frequent intervals as though he has a train to catch. 'Need some help with that?' he snaps.

With a trembling hand, Owen quickly places a tick in two of the boxes, scribbles his signature on the dotted line below and thrusts the document at his impatient companion.

Sebastian scans the document with rapid, darting movements of his eyes which glitter despite their dark colouring. 'Are you for real, Owen?' he growls. 'Or should that be Saint Owen? You've only ticked two of the boxes. Nobody's that perfect.'

'It says tick the appropriate boxes and I have – that's all there is,' says Owen defensively, and wonders why he is being so apologetic for having led a decent life; one untarnished by most of the sins that flesh is heir to.

'Oh, I think there is. Aren't you forgetting something?'

'Am I, what's that then?'

Sebastian grins wolfishly. 'Don't be coy, Owen. You know what I'm talking about.'

Owen stares blankly back at him. 'Your sibling... your very successful sibling?'

'My brother? What's he got to do with this?'

'Oh, I think you know where this is leading...'

'And where's that then?'

'E-N-V-Y, my dear. They've got it. You want it. ENVY! Flaunt it, don't they?'

'Who does?'

'Those that have it.' Sebastian grins broadly. 'That brother of yours and his wife for instance. You've had your nose pressed up against their window pane for years, haven't you, Owen? All those shiny new things in that big, expensive house of theirs. You'd love some of that, wouldn't you, eh?'

'No, not really. I've never gone in for ostentatious consumerism myself,' Owen, declares loftily.

Sebastian can see that he has touched on a raw nerve and presses home his advantage. 'Ostentatious consumerism indeed. Just listen to yourself, Owen. You're a man in denial. Come on, admit it, you sometimes long for the life they lead. And hey, why not? Why should he have so much, when you have so little?' He takes in Owen's shabby living room with a sweep of his hand.

Owen shifts uncomfortably in his chair. 'Well, I suppose I do sometimes think it's a bit unfair. I mean, I worked really hard at school. Stayed on for the sixth form. Got my A levels. I was the clever one. The grafter. Ashley

21

was the dunce…'

'Ash… ley, really?' Sebastian rolls the name around his tongue as if savouring it.

'Yeah, at least I got the better of him there.'

'No, I think it's a lovely name. Good for a boy or a girl.'

'See what I mean.'

Sebastian places his briefcase on a pine coffee table and seats himself in the armchair on the opposite side of the fireplace to Owen, crosses one lanky leg over the other. 'Go on. Tell me more about Ash… ley,' he purrs.

Owen can't help himself. Years of barely supressed sibling rivalry come bubbling to the surface and pour out of him like lava from an exploding volcano. 'Well, he just bunked off lessons. Never did his homework. He was always getting the cane for some prank or other. Sent him to the head myself once, when I was a prefect. He got six of the best that time.'

'You reported your own brother?' says Sebastian gleefully.

'Had to, he was late for school three days in a row,' Owen declares righteously.

'But still, your *little* brother…'

'Yeah well, he was a pain in the arse. Mummy's little favourite. If I had a pound for every time I had to give him one of my toys just to shut him up, I'd be a millionaire. "*I want. I want,*" that's all you ever heard from our Ashley. Funny thing is, he never wanted to play with the damned thing until I picked it up.'

'Oh Owen, *so* bitter and *so* twisted… I love it!' Sebastian brings a hand down on his thigh with a resounding slap and chuckles throatily. 'It's still not bad enough though, I'm afraid. You have to have committed all seven to qualify for entry. It's tedious I know, but the Boss made a deal with He who must not be mentioned and a deal's a deal.' He strokes his chin thoughtfully. 'We've only got three so far. Oh dear, this is going to be more difficult than I thought. Perhaps you should consider the other place. With your record you should have no trouble getting in upstairs.'

'I've already tried them. They didn't want to know.' Owen admits glumly.

Sebastian jumps to his feet and vigorously rubs his hands together. 'Well then, we're just going to have to put a few more stains on that unblemished character of yours. Oh, I can't believe I'm saying this Owen, but you are one of the saddest cases I've had in the last three hundred years. Prepare yourself for a bumpy ride – Uncle Sebbie is going to take you in hand!'

'Oh no,' whines Owen. 'I'd rather you didn't.'

'Trust me Owen, Sebbie knows best.' Sebastian assures him. 'But before we go, a bite to eat, I think,' he says and claps his hands.

2: A GLUTTON FOR PUNISHMENT

Owen is expecting a reprise of Sebastian's theatrical trick with the coffee, but when his visitor opens his hands, they are empty. Owen is perplexed; he was sure that Sebastian would have something up his sleeve, but it seems he is a one-trick pony after all. For a few moments more nothing happens then slowly, the room around them begins to dissolve; ceilings, walls, furniture become plastic; forming new shapes like one of Dali's melting watches. The light dims momentarily, fades up again and Owen finds himself seated in a small, intimate, and it would appear exclusive, restaurant, for when he takes a good look at his surroundings, he discovers that he and his companion are the only diners.

Each of the dozen or so tables in the oak panelled room are lit from above by a small pendant light, whose soft radiance barely extends much beyond the table, creating an atmosphere that is warm and intimate and, as far as Owen is concerned, uncomfortably romantic. He is further discomforted by the fact that he is still wearing the rumpled short-sleeved shirt and jeans from the previous day.

'How did you do that?' Owen asks in an awed whisper. 'And that other business with the coffee?'

'Party tricks Owen,' explains Sebastian with a dismissive wave of his hand, 'nothing more. Just something I do to impress the new recruits. Give them a little glimpse, a taster if you like, of what is possible when you sign up with the Boss.'

'And believe me, I am impressed,' says Owen, 'but you should have let me change into something more suitable before bringing me to a posh place like this.'

Sebastian clicks his fingers, summoning a waitress from the darker reaches of the restaurant. 'You needn't concern yourself, Owen. What you're wearing is absolutely perfect for what I have in mind.'

A familiar looking platinum blonde, dressed in a figure-hugging, gold lamé dress, approaches the table and leans into their circle of light.

'Good evening, gen'lemen. What's your pleasure?' she purrs.

Too stunned to speak, Owen can only stare and marvel at the iconic figure standing at his elbow. She is so close he can smell her perfume. Could it really be *her* or just a woman who bears a striking resemblance to the star? Is that the reason for the subdued lighting in here, he wonders?

Sebastian seems totally unfazed by the presence of this legendary figure in the restaurant or her waiting on tables. 'A bottle of the house red and oysters, lots of them, darling,' he orders with casual aplomb.

'Comin' right up,' she says and bestows a dazzling smile upon each of them then, turning to Owen, she raises an outstretched palm to her pouting red lips and blows him a kiss. Transfixed, his eyes follow her swaying hips as she sashays back across the floor until she disappears into the shadows.

'Was that Marilyn… where in hell did she come from?'

Sebastian arches an eyebrow and, as realization dawns on Owen's startled face he says, 'Give the man a cigar.'

Owen has a head full of questions, but before he can get any of them out, Sebastian embarks on another of his party tricks. Conjuring up an elegant cut-glass vase he places it in the centre of the table, then reaching behind Owen's left ear, brings forth a single, blood red rose. He repeats the process until he is holding twelve closed blooms in his left hand, and then drops them into the vase with a flourish. The instant the dozen stems hit the bottom of the vase it begins to fill with water and the blooms open up.

'Voilà!' he cries and, beaming with pleasure, stands back to admire his handiwork.

'I wish you wouldn't keep doing that,' says Owen testily.

'Why not?'

Sebastian's face darkens, and Owen instantly regrets his intemperate reaction to what was, he grudgingly admits, an impressive piece of magic. 'Because…' he falters, begins again. 'I mean, it's all very…'

He is saved from digging any deeper by the arrival of Marilyn with a bottle of wine in one hand and two glasses in the other. She sets a glass down in front of each of them and at Sebastian's insistence pours a generous quantity into both.

'Now you just sit back and enjoy your wine boys, and I'll be back with the oysters before you know it,' she says brightly and sashays back into the darkness.

Sebastian watches expectantly as Owen takes a polite sip from his wine. 'I hope the wine at least is to sir's taste,' he says tartly.

'Yes, it's fine, thank you. Very good,' Owen enthuses, eager to get back into his host's good books. 'Australian, isn't it?'

'N-o-o, it's the house wine, remember?' Sebastian pauses for effect. 'Comes from 'down below' rather than 'down under', I think you'll find.'

Owen almost chokes on the fresh mouthful of wine he has just taken then spluttering, spits it back into his glass. 'You mean, this is some kind of devil's brew?' he says when he recovers the power of speech.

'Owen, it was a joke.' Sebastian throws his head back and laughs. It's a mirthless sound and has a mocking quality; like the bark of a hyena. He picks up the bottle and examines the label. 'There, you see, it's Bulgarian.' He turns the bottle round and shows Owen the label. 'I'd better get you a fresh glass,' he says, and proceeds to produce one – from up his sleeve, the inside pocket of his jacket – Owen has no idea where it comes from – and fills it to the brim. 'Try and keep this one down, will you Owen, there's a good chap,' he says as he hands him the fresh glass.

Owen is too occupied to reply. With furrowed brow he concentrates on conveying the brimming glass safely to his lips, but his hand is trembling and he spills some of the wine; the droplets forming a blood-red trail on the crisp, virgin white tablecloth. Staring at these winey stigmata, he is reminded of his remark to Sebastian earlier about signing his name in blood and the life-and-death seriousness of the commitment he has made. He looks up from these gloomy contemplations to find Sebastian's penetrating gaze upon him.

'A penny for them, Owen,' he says, and leaning forward in his chair he places his elbows on the table, rests his chin upon his steepled fingers.

'Oh, nothing really, I was just wondering what we're doing here, that's all.'

'Really? We're sitting in a restaurant, Owen, that should give you some idea, don't you think? But now you come to mention it, there is one small matter I need to go over with you before the food arrives.'

Owen's face drops at the thought of further complications.

'Don't look so alarmed. It's nothing really, just one of those tedious clauses that we skipped over earlier.'

Owen notes the use of the plural, *"we"*. As if Sebastian had given him any choice in the matter, but he knows by now that it would be useless to argue the point – it's too late for that anyway, he has already signed the contract.

'You see, Owen, the Boss is running what is known as a pyramid scheme – do you know how that works?'

Owen sighs. 'I have a vague, idea but aren't those schemes illegal?'

This brings a wry smile to Sebastian's lips. 'In your world, Owen perhaps, but...' he gives a Gallic shrug of the shoulders, leaves the rest of the sentence hanging in the air. 'It's very simple. I recruit you, and you in turn recruit someone else.' Owen is about to protest but Sebastian forestalls him with a wave of his hand. 'Don't worry, I'm not expecting you to go knocking on doors or accosting people in the street. It will all be laid on for you. Name, address... everything you need to know, and of course, you will receive full training from yours truly. As it happens, I have a suitable candidate all lined up and ready to go.'

'Oh no, do I have to...? I'm no good at selling. I'll only mess it up,' says Owen. 'Who is it anyway? Is it someone I know?'

'All in good time, Owen, but first we need to tick a few more of those little boxes. Ah, at last, the Oysters,' he cries with boyish delight, as a smiling Marilyn presents Owen with a huge plate of the edible molluscs. 'Hmmm... the food of love,' says Sebastian in rapturous tones. 'That lot will put some ink in your pen, eh Owen?'

'Oh, you boys,' sighs Marilyn and giggling, returns to her station.

'So, how long has it been?' Sebastian asks, once Marilyn is out of earshot.

Owen, who has not eaten oysters before, is eying the gristly looking bodies lying in their half shells with some trepidation. He prods at one of them with the tiny fork provided and it shivers in its watery bed. 'What do you mean, how long? How long since what, exactly?'

'Since you had sex?' With someone other than yourself, that is.' He adds, with a knowing wink.

'Oh, I don't know,' Owen's face reddens. 'It's been a while, I guess.'

'Exactly how long is a while?' Sebastian enquires, and taking up his glass he takes a sip.

Owen has to think hard before replying, 'Two... maybe three, years?'

It's Sebastian's turn to almost choke on his wine. 'Three years without a shag!,' he splutters, 'You must be gagging for it.'

'Oh, you get used to it after a while.'

'Used to it?' Sebastian laughs his hyena laugh. 'Might as well shave your head and call yourself Brother Owen!' He begins to sing, 'Oh bro-ther, oh bro-ther...' in a passable impression of a boy chorister.

Owen leaps to his feet and tearing the napkin from his throat, throws it down on the table. 'Oh, thanks very much. So glad we had this little chat, Sebastian. It's done wonders for my self-esteem!'

Sebastian ceases chanting and rising, gently pushes Owen back down in his seat. 'Owen, I'm so sorry. No really, I mean it,' he adds when Owen looks doubtful. 'I had no idea you were such a sensitive soul. When the time comes to decide on a new career for you, I think we should give the arts some serious consideration. How do you fancy becoming a famous artist or poet?'

His anger mollified somewhat by Sebastian's fulsome apology, Owen retrieves his napkin and tucks it back into the top of his shirt. 'I was an artist of sorts in my last job,' he says.

'Oh really?' Sebastian picks up the bottle of wine, tops up his glass, and sits down.

'Yeah, after I was made redundant I did a bit of painting and decorating, just to keep a bit of cash rolling in. Painted the railings at the local parish church – St.

Biddulph's – do you know it?'

'Yes, I know it. Not exactly the Sistine Chapel though, is it.'

'I'm no Michelangelo,' Owen counters and Sebastian smiles.

'He's with *us*, actually.' Sebastian says proudly.

'No. Michelangelo? You're kidding!'

'I kid you not. A lot of artists and writers sign up with the Boss.'

'Why's that then?'

'It's obvious, isn't it?'

'Oh, because they're gay, you mean.'

Sebastian's dark eyes glow like hot coals and the walls around them ripple as if they are no more substantial than painted canvas flats. Owen blinks and when he looks again, everything is as it was before, and he wonders if he imagined it. 'Some are, some aren't. Doesn't mean they're bad people. A trifle homophobic, aren't we, Owen. Why is that, I wonder?'

'Meaning what, exactly?'

'No matter, we were discussing the great and the good. Immortality is what they crave; a burning desire to leave their mark on a largely uncaring world. It's hard for them, poor dears. They all want it, but so few can achieve it. That's when they turn to us. Michelangelo was so jealous of da Vinci, he wanted us to destroy his rival's work. Erase it completely. We managed to get some of the sculptures and a few of the frescos, but a lot of the paintings and drawings survived. I suspect a spot of divine intervention myself. They were mainly religious works, after all.'

Owen is outraged. 'Those were masterpieces! How

could you destroy great works of art like that?'

For his part Sebastian seems bemused by Owen's outburst. 'A deal's a deal. You sign, we deliver… anything, and I do mean *anything,* you desire.'

'All the same…'

'We're not the Boy Scouts, Owen,' Sebastian snaps. 'You called us, remember?'

'So?'

'So, you're in no position to start moralising.' He sighs; a sign of impatience or is it regret? Owen is unable to decide which. 'Without our help, Michelangelo would have remained an obscure painter of the Italian School, and the beauty you seem to care so much about would not have seen the light of day.'

'The end justifies the means, is that it? What about da Vinci?'

'What about da Vinci? The Mona Lisa's probably the most reproduced work in the history of art. Food for thought, eh?' He eyes Owen's untouched plate. 'Talking of which, you haven't touched those oysters yet. Get those down you, you're going to need them. It's obvious from what you've told me that you're woefully unready for the task I have planned for you, and after three years without a mount, so to speak, we need to get you back in the saddle as soon as possible. Owen, are you listening to me?'

Owen is still worrying over his plate of oysters. Should he spear the damn things with the tiny fork or simply suck them bodily from their shells? 'How do you eat these things?' he whispers, his embarrassment clear in his red face.

'Ah, I see,' says Sebastian, 'It's your first time.' He smiles indulgently. 'Well, it's quite simple. You loosen the little darlings from their shells with the fork, then you pick up the shell and slurp the oyster down, but be sure you chew it once or twice before swallowing, or you won't get the full flavour.'

Owen remains doubtful. 'Do you think I could have something else? Only I'm not that keen on fish of any kind.'

'Don't be such a faint heart. Eat and enjoy. I had them specially flown in for you.'

While a stern-faced Sebastian looks on, Owen, feeling much like his boyhood self when his mother had insisted that he eat his greens, loosens one of the oysters and, raising the shell to his mouth, tips the gristly morsel in. As instructed, he chews it twice before swallowing. It tastes very salty and vaguely fishy, but otherwise not as unpleasant as he had expected. Further courses follow along with more wine and by the end of the evening Owen is slowly sliding under the table weighed down by the vast amounts of food and drink he has put away.

'You know, this Bulgarian Merlot isn't half bad,' Sebastian observes as he tops up his glass. 'I must tell the Boss. He's partial to a drop of the red stuff. The redder the better and served at room temperature.' He smiles enigmatically as though enjoying a private joke. 'More vino, Owen?' he asks, and glancing across at his companion sees him slip off his chair and onto the floor. Sebastian puts his feet up on the chair Owen has vacated. 'Well, I think that takes care of gluttony,' he says and laughing, raises his glass, 'Here's to lust!' he toasts.

Flat out on the floor, Owen begins to snore loudly.

3: LAP DANCING IN THE DARK

Owen's transition from sleep to wakefulness is sudden and painful. Like a man who has been dropped from a great height, he lays spread-eagled, face down on the floor. When he tries to roll over, his limbs fail to respond to the brain's commands as if they are no longer connected to one another, yet every single one of them aches; vies for his immediate attention. How did he get here? What was he doing? He can't even remember coming to bed. And, why is he naked? He habitually wears pyjamas summer and winter alike.

He concentrates instead on just turning his head to one side but, as daylight enters his retina, a new pain – fiercer than all the rest put together – hits the back of his skull like a stiletto blade. This pain, however, is a familiar one; it's the regular companion to a hangover. He presumes he has spent a second night bingeing on lager, but can remember nothing of it.

What he does recall, and in vivid detail, is a weird dream he has had in which he agreed to sell his soul to a rather camp, fallen angel. In return for this precious item he would receive a successful new life in an, as yet, unspecified area of the creative arts. For reasons best known to this Sebastian character, achieving this goal had required him to eat large quantities of oysters. It was all very bizarre and unsettling, but it wasn't the first time he'd experienced nightmares like this one after a night out on the piss.

In a complicated series of manoeuvres and all the while keeping his eyes clamped shut, Owen manages to raise himself up onto his hands and knees. In this fashion he crawls out into the darkened hallway, where he judges it safe to open his eyes. Shuffling into the bathroom he relieves himself and, using the hand basin for support, finally manages to haul himself up onto two feet. Leaning over the basin he turns on the tap and cupping his hands, splashes cold water all over his face. Feeling slightly more human he straightens up to find one of Edvard Munch's screamers staring back at him from the mirror; a ghastly pastiche of his usual self with staring eyes and a gaping mouth. 'When will I ever learn?' he mutters to himself and, staggering back to the bedroom, he flops down onto the bed and before long is fast asleep once more.

He is woken some time later by the persistent ringing of a bell. It takes him a while to realise that it's his own front doorbell he can hear. Someone is pressing on it continuously. Cursing his impatient caller, Owen jumps out of bed and grabbing his dressing gown from the hook behind the door, hastily pulls it on and stomps downstairs.

'Alright, alright, I'm coming. Keep your hair on,' he shouts. 'For crying out loud!' he adds, as the bell continues to ring. He throws open the door to be confronted by the 'fallen angel' from his bizarre dream. He has swapped the Savile Row suit for an open-necked Ralph Lauren shirt and cream chinos, but there's no mistaking those sculpted cheek bones and swept back, black hair, it's Sebastian alright, and from the tightening in his gut, Owen is in no doubt at all that he has indeed sold his soul to this devil incarnate.

'What's the matter, Owen? You look as if you've seen a ghost,' observes Sebastian cheerily.

Owen glances up and down the street. 'You'd better come in,' he says, 'The neighbours will be wondering what the hell's going on with you ringing the doorbell like that, and me still in my dressing gown. What happened to walking through walls unannounced?' he asks, as he closes the door behind his nattily dressed visitor.

'I made you jump, you said, so I thought it best to gain admittance in a more appropriate manner. What *will* the neighbours be thinking, by the way?'

'That you're my boyfriend or worse – a rent boy! Too late now, anyway,' says Owen grumpily. Glancing over his shoulder, he is surprised to discover that Sebastian is no longer there. He stoops to peer through the bannisters but can't see him in the narrow hallway either, and assumes his visitor has already made his way to the lounge. When Owen starts back up again, it's to find Sebastian blocking his way.

'Really? And what would you know about those?' he says, with a wolfish grin. 'I do believe naughty Owen has been holding out on Uncle Sebbie?'

'Okay, let's get something straight, I'm not gay!' Owen declares, his face reddening, 'Got it?'

'So, why are you taking me to your bedroom,

darling?'

'Oh hell!' Owen does a quick about turn and scrambles back downstairs as fast as his skinny legs will carry him. Planting himself at the foot of the stairwell, he beckons Sebastian to come down. 'I was going upstairs to get washed and dressed. You were supposed to take yourself off to the living room,' he explains between gasps for breath.

Hands on hips, Sebastian slinks down the stairs like a fashion supermodel parading on a grand staircase or catwalk. Owen meanwhile follows his progress with nervous apprehension. It's like watching a big cat – fascinating but dangerous when they get too close, and Owen flinches when Sebastian places a hand on his shoulder. 'Oh Owen, you're so easy to wind up,' he purrs, as he passes along the hallway on his way to Owen's shabby living room.

Suppressing a shudder, Owen starts back up the stairs to the accompaniment of Sebastian's mocking laughter. He pauses on the landing and leaning over the bannisters, checks that Sebastian hasn't doubled back and followed him up. 'You've really dropped yourself in it this time, Owen,' he tells himself. Grabbing a towel from the airing cupboard on the landing, he wastes no time in getting to the bathroom. Once safely inside he bolts the door before stripping off and getting under the shower, where he lingers for some time beneath the cascading droplets; luxuriating in their warm caress and the reviving effect this has on his tired body. Refreshed, he dries himself and then shaves. By the time he has finished, the face in the mirror looks more or less recognizable as his once more.

In his bedroom, which is only slightly less dowdy than the living room below it, Owen pulls on some fresh clothes; a black Tee shirt with the Guinness logo emblazoned across the chest and his only other pair of jeans. He carefully closes the wardrobe door which hangs precariously on one hinge; the other having succumbed to the ravages of rust and broken off some years before. It's then that he spots the clothes he was wearing the previous day which someone has neatly folded and placed on the pine chair which stands in front of the bay window. Owen is not by nature or inclination a folder of clothes or plumper-up of cushions, but is on his own admission a bit of a slob. This sudden attack of tidiness has him puzzled until the awful truth dawns on him; it was Sebastian who had brought him home, undressed him, and put him to bed. And it was the fastidious Mr Sebastian who had afterwards neatly folded his clothes and carefully placed them on the chair.

This disturbing sequence of events runs through Owen's head like a looped video, but it's all conjecture; he has a vague memory of being in a restaurant and of Sebastian plying him with oysters but what happened after that is a blank. It's his imagination which is joining up the dots to form these flickering images that disturb him so much. Fragments are all he really has to go on and the neatly folded pile of clothes, but the thought that Sebastian had had him naked and at his mercy just won't go away. Owen knows he is being irrational; that he is letting his personal prejudices colour his judgement. He can almost hear Sebastian laughing and saying, 'You should be so lucky, dear.' But irrational or not, the thought worries him. He could of course ask the direct question, but Sebastian obviously enjoys winding him up, and will take full advantage of any opportunity he provides him with to play on these fears of his. He can't afford to forget that, despite Sebastian's outward charm, he is the devil's agent and is no doubt capable of just about anything by way of retribution if pushed far enough.

Owen straps on his Rotary watch – a 21st Birthday present from his parents – and is shocked to discover that it's six-thirty, but is it morning or evening? Crossing to the window, he pulls back the yellowed curtains. The sun hangs low over the Birmingham skyline; a smouldering red ball – it is setting not rising and Owen realises he has almost slept the clock around.

When he joins Sebastian downstairs he finds him standing in front of the bay window. The setting sun glows redly in the glass behind him like the fires of hell itself. When he turns and fixes his dark gaze on Owen it's almost as if the devil can read his mind.

'So tell me, why are you so homophobic Owen, hmm?'

'I'm not. I just wanted to make it crystal clear which side I'm batting for,' he says defiantly.

'Yet you flinched when I put my hand on your shoulder earlier.'

'You made me jump, that's all.'

It's clear from the quizzical look that Sebastian gives him that A: he doesn't accept this explanation and B: he didn't need to ask the question; he already knows all there is to know about Owen and his life. He is just playing with him like a cat plays with a dead mouse. 'Granted you're wound tighter than a piggy wig's' tail, Owen, but I think we both know there's more to it than that. Well?'

'Why can't you just let it go? What's the point of asking questions when you already know the answers?'

The fiery glow at Sebastian's back has darkened to a deep purple, adding a touch of the gothic to this little tableau. 'It's you who needs to let go, don't you think? That's why I want to hear you say it.'

'Say what? That that cow of a wife of mine ran off with another woman. There, I've said it. Are you happy now?'

'Be honest, would you feel any better about her going if she had left you for another man?'

Owen considers this for a moment. Would he? The embarrassment of his wife becoming a lesbian aside, would her rejection of his love have been any less painful if she had chosen to be with another man, rather than another woman. Would the heartache and loneliness he has endured have been any easier to bear? It was hard to be certain, but he doubted if it would have made much difference and admits as much to Sebastian.

'Then your wife's sexual orientation doesn't come into it. Bottom line is, she preferred to be with someone else. Let it go... let *her* go. You're trouble is you take life far too seriously. You need to lighten up, live a little... have some fun!'

The purple shadows of twilight fill the room now and Sebastian is little more than a dark silhouette, a cardboard cut-out. Owen crosses to a fluted standard lamp and switches it on. The narrow circle of light that manages to escape from beneath its heavy, parchment-thick shade alleviates the gloom in the lamp's immediate vicinity but only deepens the shadows in the further reaches of the room.

'It's true what they say; if you fall off a horse it's best to jump straight back into the saddle,' says Sebastian and joining Owen by the fireplace, seats himself in the nearest armchair. 'So pop back upstairs and get changed. We're going out.'

'Why, what's wrong with what I'm wearing?'

Sebastian looks Owen up and down, wrinkles his nose. 'What isn't wrong with it?' he says tartly.

'Well, it would help if I knew where we were going.'

'We, my dear, are going to a lap dancing club.'

'But I can't dance,' protests Owen.

Sebastian gives him a withering look. 'Owen, *you* don't have to dance. You stuff some fivers down the knickers of one of the young ladies there and she dances for you.'

*

Owen is hiding in the gents' toilets. He has been in there for more than ten minutes now. The heavy, leather padded outer door is constantly banging as the 'gentlemen' come and go to relieve themselves at the urinal. He catches snatches of conversations, peppered with sexual swear words, and frequently accompanied by raucous laughter; the occasional fart; the explosive sound of cascading water when the urinal is cleansed, and the constant blast of hand dryers. Owen is only in here because he is desperately trying to put off the moment when he has to step back into the club Sebastian has brought him to. It's called *The Pussy Galore Club*, a lap dancing club for 'gentlemen'. The façade is late Georgian, but the interior is early Las Vegas. Clearly a great deal of money has been spent on creating the expensive, glitzy interior but ultimately the effect is tawdry; more high class brothel than classy club for gentlemen.

He consults his watch; it's been fourteen minutes since he excused himself. He can't stay in here much longer or Sebastian will come looking for him and drag him out of his cubicle hiding place. This is not Owen's idea of a night out; the drinks are expensive and the stag night atmosphere, with a bunch of mainly middle-aged men paying girls young enough to be their daughters to 'bump and grind' over them in nothing more than a 'G-string' is abhorrent. And worst of all, Sebastian expects him to join in! It's embarrassing, indeed shameful and makes him feel like some dirty old pervert at a Soho peep show. It's not that Owen isn't excited, aroused even by the sight of a naked woman – he just prefers it to be on a one-to-one basis with a woman nearer his own age; someone who remembers perestroika and the night The Berlin Wall came down.

When 16 minutes have elapsed Owen flushes the toilet for form's sake and reluctantly leaves the cubicle. He spends a further 3 minutes washing and drying his hands before exiting the gents and walks straight into Sebastian who was about to enter the washroom.

'Ah Owen, there you are. I was beginning to think you'd gone to sleep in there,' he nods towards the loos. 'Or did you make an interesting new friend?' he adds with a salacious grin.

'Don't start that again,' Owen hisses through gritted teeth.

'So, what took you so long?'

'Got a gippy tummy,' he lies. 'All those oysters, I

expect.'

'If you say so,' observes Sebastian, who clearly doesn't believe him, and taking hold of the lapels of Owen's jacket, gives it a tug. It's one size too small for Owen and canary yellow.

Owen sighs. 'There's no need to rub it in, I know I look a prat.'

'It's a tad loud for my taste, I must say.'

'It's not half as loud as the music in here.' Owen is forced to shout in order to be heard above the raunchy rock music that the dozen or so bored looking girls are bumping and grinding their hips to. The lighting is more subdued in here, more intimate. The girls are dancing on tables, some performing with poles. The men seated around the tables on circular padded, leather couches stare up at the girls and, before each performance, thrust bank notes into their skimpy underwear or into the frilly garters that adorn some of their thighs.

'It's a night club Owen, what did you expect?'

'Let's just get this over with, shall we.' He waves a hand towards the bevy of gyrating females. 'Which one of those strippers is Avril?'

'They're not strippers, they're lap dancers,' Sebastian corrects him.

'It's not what I'd call it,' observes Owen primly. 'Look at that one there.' He points to a petite blonde who is wriggling on the lap of a shaven headed man who has a swallow tattooed on his neck. 'She's squirming all over his…'

'That's why it's called lap dancing.' Sebastian's dark brows come together to form a menacing V. 'It's what we came here for,' he asserts testily; 'Raw, undisguised lust.

You can almost smell the sex in here. Doesn't it make you feel randy?'

'Actually, I feel sick.'

Sebastian drapes an arm around Owen's shoulder, pulls him into a hug. 'Owen, my dear, I'm beginning to think you've been holding out on Sebbie'

Owen roughly pushes Sebastian away. 'Get off me, will you,' he says hotly. 'I've told you, I'm straight.'

'The jury's still out as far as I'm concerned.'

'And what's that supposed to mean?'

Arching an eyebrow, Sebastian's eyes slide downwards to fix on Owen's crotch, 'I mean, our little soldier isn't exactly standing to attention, is he?'

'We're not all like that lot, you know!' he says angrily, pointing at the seated men who stare fixedly, as if hypnotised by the gyrations of the near-naked girls dancing in front of them.

Taking hold of Owen's elbow, Sebastian steers him towards the nearest available table, one of the few that has remained unoccupied. 'Why don't you sit down and order some drinks. When Avril is free I'll bring her over to you.' Sebastian scans the crowded room for a moment. 'Ah, there she is,' he says, and Owen follows the line of his pointing finger to fix on an unusually tall, leggy brunette.

'Shall I save a seat for her or will she be standing on the table?'

Ignoring Owen's heavy handed sarcasm, Sebastian guides him between table and couch and pushes him down onto the padded leather. 'Relax. She won't be working again tonight. You'll have her all to yourself.'

Owen takes another look at the girl. 'Bit young for me, isn't she?'

Sebastian stares at him in mock disbelief. 'Well, there's a novelty. A middle-aged man complaining that a woman is *too* young for him. Owen, you must be unique. Most men your age would be cock-a-hoop, no pun intended, at the prospect of roggering some youthful totty. Girls like Avril are the answer to every middle-aged man's mid-life crisis. Don't you ever look on the bright side? You've been crossing the desert for ten long years. I lead you to an oasis and you refuse to slake your thirst because it's freshwater and not salt.'

'Three. It's only been three years,' Owen corrects him.

'Three... ten, what's the difference?'

'Seven years, when I was at school.'

'Whatever,' says Sebastian with undisguised impatience. 'Most men in your position would be grateful for something that walks on two legs, never mind a tasty dish like Avril.'

'That's what I mean. A girl like that isn't going to fancy me, is she?'

'Oh Lucifer, give me strength! Owen, she does it for the M-O-N-E-Y. She doesn't have to fancy you. Which reminds me...' He thrusts his right hand into a pocket of his chinos and draws out a large wad of notes. 'You'll be needing some cash,' he tells him and taking hold of Owen's hand, thrusts the folded bills into his palm, then closes his fingers around it.

'Oh great, how do you think that makes me feel?'

'Feel? Feel! Feelings don't come into it. A quick wham, bang, thank you mam, is all that's required for our purposes. You don't have to romance her.'

Owen is horrified. 'But I have to work up to it,' he

45

explains. 'I can't just go diving in at the deep end.'

Sebastian rolls his eyes. 'You're way out of your depth already, if you ask me.' He gives his reluctant protégé a fatherly pat on the shoulder. 'I won't be long. Try and contain your excitement until I get back.'

Owen watches Sebastian weave his way between the tables, set like small islands in a magenta sea; an effect created by the moody lighting in this, the main area of the club for 'dancing'. A waitress – wearing little more than the dancers themselves – appears at his elbow; offers to take his drinks order. Owen asks for lager and is told they don't serve beer in the *Pussy Galore*. He settles for cocktails for no other reason than that he finds the names amusing; *'a slow comfortable screw against the wall'* in particular, though he doesn't have the nerve to ask for it. Sebastian approaches the tall, dark haired girl and whispers something in her ear. She turns and glances towards Owen's table, nods her head, then continues dancing for the half dozen or so men in various stages of intoxication who surround her.

'Sad bastards,' Owen mutters to himself.

Sebastian begins weaving his way back towards Owen. At the same time, the topless waitress returns with the cocktails (the generic term itself is suggestive) and with a fixed smile creasing her pancake make-up, she carefully places three tall glasses of violently coloured drinks, each decorated with slices of fruit, paper parasols and a drinking straw on the table in front of Owen. It strikes him as ironic, that the girl's make-up covers a larger proportion of her skin than her scanty costume does. He thanks her and, when she continues to hover, peels off a bill from the roll Sebastian has given him and hands it to her. Apparently satisfied with the offering, she teeters off on her stiletto heels, her naked buttocks slung like saddle-bags over her G-string.

'The drinks are bloody expensive here, aren't they,' Owen says as Sebastian slides into the space beside him. 'This lot set you back the best part of fifty quid. Where is she then?'

'Patience, Owen, she'll be along in a minute.' Sebastian surveys the colourful glasses. 'Which one of these is mine,' he asks.

'Take your pick. I ordered three pints of lager but they don't serve beer in here, apparently. Waitress was quite snooty about it.'

'Such a difficult decision, they all look so tempting. Take this one for instance,' he taps one of the glasses, 'looks like a sunrise; always a good omen, don't you think? A new day; signifying a fresh start, but looked at from a different perspective, it could be a sunset which is a much more sinister analogy; representing as it does one's declining years, the end of one's life.' He makes it sound like a threat and Owen suspects that that is exactly what it's intended to be. "Br-o-wn sugar," sings Mick Jagger, and across the room Avril wraps her long thighs around a metal pole as if making love to it. Sebastian passes a finger over each of the glasses in turn. 'Eenie, meenie, miney, mo,' he chants and on mo, picks up the 'Tequila Sunrise' and takes a long suck at the straw. 'Umm, yummy,' he enthuses. 'You must try this one, Owen, it's scrumptious,' he says and offers the glass to his companion.

'No thanks. I don't have a long spoon on me.'

'You don't need a spoon, Owen. They come with a straw.'

'It's an old saying… something about needing a long spoon when you sup with the devil,' Owen explains.

'Oh, I see, must tell the Boss that one the next time I catch him in a good mood.'

'Yeah, I had a boss like that once. He was no fun at all. Bastard made me redundant.' Owen feels the old blackness coming over him; the dark mood that in the past has dragged him down into the deepest of abysses. He quickly snatches up one of the remaining cocktails; a deep blue one, the colour of a summer sky. It tastes like cough medicine and grimacing, he pushes it away from him in disgust. 'Can we go to the pub now?' he whines.

'No, Owen, we can't. I didn't bring you here to get drunk.'

'Just as well. The stuff they serve here is undrinkable.'

'Oh, get a life will you. It's no wonder you wanted to die.'

'It wasn't my idea to come here.'

'No, it was mine and may I remind you, I'm doing you a favour. If you'd led a more interesting life neither of us would have to be here.'

'I don't need your help to get a woman.'

'Fine,' says Sebastian equably, and leaning back against the padded leather, spreads his arms out across the back of the couch. With his sharply cut features he resembles a large bird of prey fanning its wings as it comes in to land. 'You're spoilt for choice here. Take your pick.' Owen shifts uncomfortably in his seat but otherwise shows no intention of making a move. 'Well, what are you waiting for? Come on, show old Sebbie how it's done.'

'Give us a chance. Haven't finished me drink.'

'You said it was undrinkable,' Sebastian reminds him.

'It's not that bad, when you get used to it. Bit like Guinness or oysters.'

'How's that?'

'You know... an acquired taste, like.'

'Two helpings of oysters didn't give you much of a taste for *them*. How is the stomach now by the way... still feeling queasy?'

'A bit. And I still say those oysters were off.'

Sebastian smiles to himself, shakes his head. 'Hardly,' he says, and gives Owen a sly, sideways glance. 'They were still tucked up in their beds in Galway Bay barely minutes before you ate them.'

'But that's not possible.'

Sebastian's unfathomably deep, dark eyes are staring directly into Owen's own now, and it feels like the devil has crawled inside him, inhabits his very soul. 'I told you Owen, anything... *absofuckinglutely* anything you desire.'

'Yes, and I believe you.' He pats his stomach. 'Must be butterflies.'

Sebastian is puzzled by Owen's reference to Lepidoptera. 'Pardon?'

'Nerves.' Owen explains, surprised by the gaps in his companion's knowledge of colloquial English. Still, he did have a foreign sounding surname so perhaps English wasn't his first language. 'I've never done anything like this before. Gone on a blind date, I mean. I still think she's much too young for me.'

'It's too late to back out now, here she comes. When she offers you a private dance, you just say yes. Got it?'

'Yes, okay!' Owen looks up to see Avril striding towards them. Closer to, she looks even younger than she did from a distance, and is far prettier than he'd expected.

She has a wide, generous mouth with lips that have a permanent look of having just been crushed by a kiss. Her eyes are hazel and flecked with amber hi-lights. When she speaks, Owen detects traces of a northern accent; from Manchester or Leeds perhaps? She is also several inches taller than Owen. Her youth and looks alone would be enough to intimidate him.

Within minutes of sitting down and being introduced, Avril had suggested that she and Owen should adjourn to one of the private suites that opened off the main room. "We'll be more comfortable there," she'd assured him. In a way it had been a welcome relief; a chance to get away from his tormentor, but now that he is alone with the girl, all he wants is to get away from her too. The short walk from their table to the 'Topaz Suite' has taken Owen way outside his comfort zone. He has no previous experience to draw on; has never paid a woman to have sex with him before. But it isn't sex he can smell in here, it's desperation; his own and that of the other men who have been here before him. He wonders how many times a night Avril becomes someone's 'Private Dancer' for money.

The girl is going through what he presumes is her 'foreplay' routine; draping herself over the padded leather couch, parading around the room in her high heels like a catwalk model, but it's her body, not what she is wearing, that is on show. Though his desire to run is greater than any desire he might have for her, Owen can't help looking at her. The way she moves fascinates him as she prowls about the room like a big cat. Just like Sebastian earlier, he recalls with a shudder, and frantically searches the dimly lit room for a way out. Essentially, it's a miniature version of the main room; the same subdued lighting, the same circular table and same padded leather couch.

'Is there a back door out of here?' he asks hopefully.

The girl laughs. 'Sebastian said you were highly strung. No, there isn't.'

Owen's heart sinks. What to do now? 'Do you mind if we just talk?' he suggests.

'It's your money…'

'Actually, it's Sebastian's.'

'You should have said. I would have charged *him* double.' She laughs throatily; a surprisingly deep sound from such a slim frame.

Owen laughs briefly in return, but then falls silent. Having said he wants to talk, he can think of nothing to say; finds himself wishing the girl would come up with a suitable topic. But what is a suitable topic for conversation in these circumstances. In the awkward silence that follows the only sounds are the girl's breathing and the insistent beat of the bass line coming from the other room. It pulses like a heartbeat in the background or is it his own heart he can hear sounding in his ears?

'They usually talk about their wives,' Avril prompts. 'Do you want to talk about your wife?'

'Maureen. Her name was Maureen.'

'Was? Does that mean she's dead?'

'No, no. She's still alive. She ran off with another woman.'

'Ah, decided she *was* a lesbian after all, did she?'

Owen had not thought about Maureen in those terms before, had not classified her as such. 'I suppose so. Yes,' he agrees, and then falls silent again. The seconds tick by until Owen can stand it no longer. 'Look, no offence

April…'

'Avril,' she corrects him.

'*Avril,* sorry, I do apologise, but this entire evening's been a terrible mistake,' he admits, dropping all pretence. 'I didn't want to come here. It was Sebastian's idea.'

'I know. He's full of bright ideas, that one,' says Avril matter-of-factly, but Owen has jumped to his feet and is heading for the door. 'Hey! Where do you think you're going buster?' she shouts after him.

His hand already reaching for the door handle, Owen turns, 'Home. This stupid business has gone far enough.'

In three strides of her long legs, Avril is standing beside him and has her foot pressed hard against the door. 'Oh no you don't. You think this is a game, you stupid, little man?' she hisses through clenched teeth. 'You signed a contract, and take it from someone who knows, Sebastian will hold you to every last dotted-i and crossed-t of it. You walk out of here and there will be serious consequences, and not just for you either. My son's future depends on me keeping my end of the bargain. So, if you know what's good for you, you'll get your arse back on that couch because it belongs to Sebastian now. Mine too, and he doesn't take any bloody prisoners!'

Her cheeks are flushed with anger and her eyes burn with a kind of madness. Faced with such ferocity, and the fear that lies behind it, Owen too grows fearful as he begins to appreciate the gravity of the situation that, thanks to his drunken folly, he has put himself in.

She is as trapped as I am, Owen realises; a beautiful butterfly being slowly devoured by one of those carnivorous plants; Venus Fly-traps they were called, weren't they? There was clearly nothing to be gained by resisting and everything to be lost. 'It's a case of *do or die*, then?' he says.

'*Exactly.*' She takes his hand in hers and leads him back to the leather couch. 'So you might as well enjoy it. You do like girls, don't you?'

Owen wants to scream. Not her as well, or did Sebastian put her up to it? Instead he says, 'Yes, of course, I do. It's not that, it's… Oh, I dunno, this way just seems a bit… well, cold-blooded for want of a better word.'

'So, pretend I'm your girlfriend or your favourite film star. I can be anyone you want me to be,' Avril suggests, and pushes him down onto the padded leather. With the expertise that comes with much practice, she quickly unbuckles his trouser belt and unzips his fly. As her slender fingers curl around the shaft, he feels his cock harden. Avril cups her other hand under his balls and gives them an encouraging squeeze. Owen moans and unlike her, he is not faking it. Her head comes down into his lap, and her long black hair spills over his belly. When her warm, soft lips close around his unyielding flesh, Owen loses the battle and lust triumphs over any moral objections he may have entertained, when he first walked into the club.

4: FRIENDS IN HIGH PLACES

Below them, a deal too far below them for Owen's peace of mind, the twinkling lights of the bars and restaurants of Brindley Place glimmer like fallen stars in the dark water of the Birmingham Canal. He and Sebastian are standing on the roof of the Hyatt Regency. Sebastian has brought him up here, or rather transported him, for one minute they were standing outside *The Pussy Galore Club*, the next they were perched on the hotel's roof like a couple of super heroes – Batman and Robin, or... unable to recall another dynamic duo, Owen abandons the search for further analogies. Besides, it requires all his concentration just to stay on his feet; there's a stiff breeze blowing up here and they are standing perilously close to the edge.

Sebastian has yet to reveal the reason for this little excursion to the roof of one of Birmingham's highest buildings but, if his intention is to scare him, then he has already succeeded; Owen has a morbid fear of falling and often has nightmares about it. He read somewhere once that a falling dream is your subconscious mind alerting you to a situation in your waking life which has got out of control. He allows himself a wry smile; as of yesterday, just about everything in his waking life seems to be out of control. He glances across at the 'puppet master' responsible for this loss of jurisdiction over his own destiny. Sebastian stands as still as a statue, his slick, black mane unruffled by the wind. Then, he has no need to fear a fall; he has already 'fallen' and where angels fear to tread, Owen must follow, but he is not ready to jump just yet.

He wonders what the dark angel has promised Avril that makes her prepared to demean herself like that night after night. Her ministrations brought him some release from years of sexual tension, but only momentarily. Owen's life has not significantly changed; when he makes his way home later, it will be to an empty house and a cold bed.

Sebastian becomes aware of Owen's gaze. 'I suppose you're wondering why I brought you up here.'

'A suicide pact – we hold hands and jump together?'

'Well, you've certainly perked up a bit. I assume we have Avril to thank for that,' Sebastian observes drily. 'But no, I want you to take a look at those dots down there.'

'Do I have to, I'm freezing my nuts off and I'm scared of heights.'

'Fear not Owen; if you should happen to slip, I'll make sure you don't hit the ground too hard.' Sebastian assures him with a wry smile.

'Thanks. That's very… reassuring.' Steeling himself, Owen leans over the edge and peers down at the tiny dots milling about below. They pour out of the bars and restaurants; criss-cross the bridge over the canal that connects Brindley Place with The International Conference Centre and Symphony Hall. 'What about them?'

'If I were to take one of those dots; that one there for instance,' he points to a beige coloured dot in the centre of the bridge. 'Wipe it from the face of the earth, would you miss him or her?'

'You're not going to, are you?'
Sebastian sighs. 'Of course not, it's a hypothetical question. But supposing…'

'Well no… I mean, I don't know any of them, but I would be sorry…'

'Precisely, you don't know them. And if I were to throw you off this roof – again, hypothetically – would any of *them* miss you?'

Owen doubts that his neighbours would miss him, let alone the faceless revellers below. He shakes his head.

'And that's why your life is so shit Owen… you're just one of the herd. You're invisible, but not for much longer.' Sebastian gives him a hearty slap on the back and Owen topples forward.

For one brief moment, Owen is convinced he can fly; that Sebastian is somehow holding him up as he floats out over the abyss, but then his heels come up above his head and he plunges earthwards. He screams, but his cry is snatched away by the wind and the moving dots below remain blissfully unaware of the ten stone bag of blood and guts on its way down to them. He knows his speed is doubling with every second and yet he seems to be falling in slow motion; has the time to consider whether Sebastian planned all along to push him off the roof or not. A trick of the mind, an illusion; the pull of gravity and the height he is falling from will determine the time it takes him to reach the ground, not Sebastian.

The dots below sprout arms and legs; become recognisably human; he can even distinguish male from female. It can't be long now before he crashes into their midst; becomes a bloody mess, a red dot on the concrete, unless he lands in the canal. The canal would be best, he decides; far preferable to go out with a nice big splash than a dull splat. Owen is painfully aware that he is going to die either way, but somehow the manner of his going has suddenly become important to him. Owen waggles his arms and legs about in a desperate attempt to steer himself towards the canal and the chance of a splash landing. He has seen gaggles of sky divers do it in video footage on YouTube, and they made it look easy, but his clumsy manoeuvres effect no visible change in his trajectory, and he continues to fall almost vertically. With impact fast approaching Owen closes his eyes tight shut and fervently hopes that death, when it comes, will be instantaneous.

He still has his eyes shut when a strong pair of hands grip him under his armpits and haul him to his feet. Owen opens his eyes to find he is standing in a paved piazza at the side of a bubbling fountain, whose wind-blown spray splatters the steps he is standing on. At his shoulder Sebastian fusses over him, brushing the dust off his gaudy jacket with sharp flicks of his long, slim fingers.

'I don't know why I'm bothering with this,' Sebastian says, and ceases his brushing. 'You should take this awful jacket back to the charity shop you bought it from and demand a refund.'

'Never mind that – what the hell happened?'

'You fainted, old love.'

'I mean before that. Why did you push me off the roof? I could have been killed.'

'Oh Owen, don't be such a drama queen. I caught you before you hit the ground, didn't I?'

'I could have had a fucking heart attack before I ever reached the ground, you mad bastard!' Owen screams at him. He begins to shake uncontrollably, and falling to his knees, is violently sick. Passers-by, assuming he is just another drunken binger, frown in disapproval; give him a wide birth.

Sebastian helps him to his feet once more, hands him a silk handkerchief. 'Here, wipe your face, you look dreadful,' he says. 'What you need is a good, stiff drink and I know just the place.'

Too weak to protest, Owen meekly allows Sebastian to lead him away to a quiet booth in a private club, whose distinguished looking members treat the dark angel with solicitous respect. On their arrival, a po-faced flunky in a fancy waistcoat helps Owen remove his vomit-stained jacket and hands him a black, single breasted-dinner jacket.

A waiter approaches and Sebastian orders two double brandies. They sit in silence until the drinks arrive. Owen gulps half of his glass down in one swallow. The fiery liquor slowly spreads its warmth throughout his body and he feels a little better; regains some of his lost composure.

'So, why did you throw me off that building?' Owen asks at last. 'What was the point, other than to scare me shitless?'

Sebastian gives him a sharp look. 'But that *was* the point. You were wavering, Owen.'

'But I did everything you asked,' Owen whines.

'*Oh please!* Don't waste my time. I know exactly what went on between you and Avril.'

'She told you?' Owen isn't that surprised, but still feels betrayed.

'She didn't have to. You underestimate my powers, little man. Just take this as your final warning and don't think of running out on me again. Besides we're not done with lust yet.'

'But, I thought…'

'You thought what… that box is ticked? I thought I'd made it abundantly clear that Avril was going to be a warm up for the main event. You really didn't think it was going to be that easy, did you? My dear Owen, you can't expect to have *everything* handed to you on a plate.'

What was the point in selling his soul then, if not to have the good life handed to him on a plate? Owen takes another gulp of brandy. He is beginning to wish he'd been left to nose-dive into the canal after all. Hell itself couldn't be much worse than the nightmare his life has become since signing that damned contract of Sebastian's. If Avril had been the starter, what had Sebastian got in mind for the main course? He was almost afraid to ask, but his curiosity got the better of him. That was the trouble with being a pessimist, he decided, you always wanted to hear the bad news first.

'So what have you got lined up for me this time?' he asks, 'or should that be who?' and swilling the last of the brandy around his glass, swallows it down.

'All in good time, Owen, but first…' Sebastian snaps his fingers and almost immediately a waiter carrying a silver tray appears at their table. 'Two more of these please,' he says, indicating the empty brandy glasses.

'Certainly sir,' replies the obsequious waiter and, placing the dirty glasses on the tray, scurries away to fetch their order.

'I don't want another drink,' Owen says petulantly, 'I just want to go home.'

'Nonsense. The night is young. Besides, you're still in shock. You need another brandy to steady your nerves.'

Owen gives a derisive snort, 'And whose fault is that? You just shoved me off a 250 foot high building. Did you think I'd just go zooming up into the air like fucking Superman, perform a few aerial stunts and then make a perfect three point landing?'

'Bravo!' Sebastian claps his hands in delight. 'That's what I like to see, a client showing a bit of spunk. Good for you.' A few elderly gentlemen's heads turn in their direction; give them disapproving looks.

Emboldened by Sebastian's approval Owen presses home his advantage. 'And I still think you should take lust off the list,' he rasps. 'It's only fair after what I've been through.'

The obsequious waiter returns and Sebastian waits until he has gone back to his station before replying. 'No can do, Owen, I'm afraid. Lust must remain on the 'to do' list for the time being. But I think we can take sloth as read, don't you?

'You're saying I'm lazy?' Owen is offended.

'I'm not just saying it, Owen, it's self-evident,' he insists and counts the points off on his fingers as he makes them. 'One, you haven't worked for several years.'

'That's not my fault. I was made redundant…'

'Two,' he continues, ignoring Owen's intervention. 'That house of yours hasn't been decorated for a decade –

no, two decades judging by the wallpaper in your lounge. Three, the garden is so overgrown it's likely to be designated a site of special scientific interest. I could go on…'

But Owen shakes his head, feels ashamed. It comes as a shock to him that he hasn't seen it himself; that he has grown so used to his surroundings, he just hasn't noticed the years of neglect and that it has taken an outsider to point it out to him.

'So that just leaves lust and greed to complete,' says Sebastian in summation.

'But greed and gluttony is the same thing, isn't it?'

'You would think so wouldn't you, but no, gluttony is eating more than you need to, whereas greed – avarice is probably a better word for it – is an excessive desire for material possessions. Not something you're guilty of, old love, but still, give it time, eh?' He rubs his hands together. 'Oh, I do love a bit of good old fashioned corruption,' he says gleefully.

'So, come on then, what is it? What have I got to do?'

Sebastian bats the enquiry away with a wave of his hand. 'Oh don't worry about the details; I'll e-mail them to you in a day or two. I'm not absolutely convinced you're up to the task yet.'

'You're going to e-mail them to me?'

'You do have a computer, don't you?'

'Well, yes of course. I just didn't expect *you* to be using one.'

'What did you think I was going to do? Send them round engraved on tablets of stone? We have to keep up with the times same as any other organization. The Boss loves his iPad; got quite a following on Twitter –

under an assumed name, of course.'

The revelation that 'Old Nick' had an iPad and 'tweeted' just seemed so incongruous to Owen that he wanted to laugh out loud, but contained himself. After all, if he could be thrown off The Hyatt rooftop by one of his minions simply for 'wavering' over the terms of his contract, where would his lord and master draw the line? Another thought occurred to him.

'Don't things like iPads... well, you know... melt down there?'

Sebastian gives him a pitying look. 'You're referring to the fires of hell, presumably. Bit of a myth that one, to be honest, put about by the competition; but obviously he can only use an iPad when in his human form, and has access to broadband. You really can be a bit dim at times you know, Owen.'

'So, I could have walked past him in the street without knowing it?'

'He doesn't wear a 'Look out, the Devil's about' tee-shirt, if that's what you mean,' Sebastian says scornfully.

Chastened, his face burning with embarrassment, Owen falls silent and nursing his brandy glass, is lost in his own thoughts.

'Oh, now she's sulking,' taunts Sebastian.

Owen can contain himself no longer. 'A couple of days ago I thought my life couldn't get any worse, but then you turned up and guess what? It has!' He jumps to his feet with every intention of storming out, but his involuntary leap from The Hyatt still fresh in his mind, quickly sits down again.

'Lesson learned I see. Good. Carrot and stick, Owen. Carrot and stick, that's the name of the game here, but this job is so much more enjoyable when I'm handing out the treats s-o-o, how do you fancy a spot of R & R in the country this coming weekend, umm? You and me, hob-knobbing with the Lords and Ladies of the County Set, what do you think?'

'Oh, I don't think so. I mean, look at me, I'd stick out like a sore thumb amongst that lot.'

'Nonsense! It will provide you with a unique opportunity to do some networking with some very influential people.' He taps the side of his nose with a forefinger. 'And don't worry, you can leave all the arrangements to me. I'll make sure you're kitted out with all the right gear'

What a strange mixture Sebastian is, thinks Owen; mailed fist one minute, kid gloves the next. Which one was the real Sebastian, he wondered? Could the dark angel truly have a good side, or was he simply drawing Owen in; making him feel dependent in the same way hostages were supposed to be drawn to their captors?

*

Friday morning Owen, still in pyjamas and dressing gown, is absent-mindedly munching toast whilst watching daytime TV when the front door bell rings. He goes to the door expecting to find the postman or a couple of Jehovah's Witnesses standing on his doorstep – the latter always came in twos – why is that, he wonders? Safety in numbers he supposes. But when he opens the door he finds two expensive looking suitcases have been left on his doorstep. He is still puzzling over them when he hears the front gate latch and looking up, sees a uniformed chauffeur striding towards him with a further suitcase and several of those covers that hire companies supply suits in, draped over one arm. At the curb is a shiny new, black Range Rover.

'Mister Tantalus sends his compliments sir, and would you be ready to leave at six o'clock this evening?' He has piercing blue eyes, a long, narrow nose and a crinkly mouth.

'Six o'clock,' Owen repeats mechanically.

'Problem, sir?'

'No, no I'll be ready, er…' had the man given his name? He couldn't remember hearing it.

'I'm Marlow, sir,' the chauffeur says and picks up one of the suitcases. 'Would you like me to come in and lay the clothes out for you?'

'Oh, that won't be necessary,' Owen assures him.

'I'll just bring these things into the hall and leave you to it then, sir.' Owen steps aside and the man carries the suitcase into the hall. 'Do you want them taking upstairs, sir?' he enquires, with a nod towards the landing.

'N-o, you're alright. Just pop them down there,' Owen tells him and points to an area of the hallway dominated by his mother's old umbrella stand. His bedroom is a tip and he has no desire to expose it to the critical gaze of this paragon of neatness; the chauffeur's blue/grey uniform is immaculate, and his black shoes polished to a mirror-like finish. The man's manner and bearing have all the hallmarks of an ex-military man and Owen, who has no enthusiasm for this sort of obsessive grooming, finds it intimidating.

'Right you are, sir. I'll just fetch the other case in,' the chauffeur says and smartly wheels about.

As soon as the man turns his back on him, Owen runs to the kitchen and begins frantically searching his jacket pockets for some loose change. To save time he spreads the money out on the kitchen table, and scooping up a few pound coins, dashes back to the front door. The chauffeur is bent over, carefully rearranging the suit covers over the three cases. When he straightens up, Owen quickly grabs one of the chauffeur's hands and presses the coins into it.

'There's no need for that, sir, we both work for Mister Tantalus, in a manner of speaking,' says the chauffeur, handing the coins back to the blushing tipper.

Mortified by his embarrassing faux pas, Owen wishes he could pause and rewind his life like a DVD, and re-run the last few minutes of it. If he can get it so wrong with a chauffeur, how is he going to manage with a bunch of toffs? Many of them would no doubt have men like Marlow working for them; affording Owen numerous opportunities to embarrass himself still further. The weekend ahead would have him floundering way outside his comfort zone, but that was nothing compared to how uncomfortable Sebastian would make things for him, if he tried to back out of it. There was nothing for it but to go and hope he didn't make too big a fool of himself. With any luck Sebastian would quickly realise his mistake in taking Owen to meet his rich friends and they would make their excuses and leave early.

'Right, I'll be off then, sir.' Marlow touches a hand to the shiny peak of his chauffeur's cap.

Startled, Owen is pulled back into the present. 'Okay, thank you,' he mutters and shows the man out. Marlow marches down the path like a guardsman on parade and at the front gate, turns and throws Owen another salute. Owen returns the salute with a self-conscious wave and, closing the door falls back against it. 'C-H-R-I-S-T!' The blasphemy bursts out of him in a great exhalation of breath. It's only then that Owen realises he has been holding it in.

The suitcases are real leather, expensive and heavy. Puffing and panting, Owen lugs them and the garment bags upstairs. Dumping the lot on his bed, he sits down heavily beside them. He is so out of condition that for the first time in his life Owen contemplates joining a gym, but on reflection, decides that the last two evenings with Sebastian would be enough to wreck the constitution of all but the most obsessive of fitness fanatics.

Recovered from his exertions, Owen pulls the nearest of the cases towards him and releases the catches. Raising the lid, he rummages through the contents, pulling out casual shirts, slacks and socks, all of them bearing Savile Row labels. Soon Owen's bedroom resembles Santa's grotto. It's like all his Christmases have arrived at once; the cases are crammed with expensive goodies; fashionable sweaters, hand-made leather shoes, tweeds and outdoor wear – everything in fact that a gentleman requires for a country house weekend. The suitcases and garment bags emptied, the bedspread is buried beneath thousands of pounds worth of top-of-the-range gents' clothing. Owen is overwhelmed by the number of purchases and the expense involved; he has never had so many clothes to choose from before, let alone garments of this quality. The frowzy bedroom is filled with the colours and heady scents of sheer luxury – the animal smells of real leather and pure wool; the peaty tang of tweed. He can't stop handling them, feeling their softness against his skin, sniffing them. But when his euphoria finally subsides, Owen realises that in his eagerness to explore the contents of the cases, he has created a knotty problem for himself; that is, how to repack them without everything getting creased. The prospect of spending a long weekend in the company of the rich and powerful is intimidating enough for a working class boy like Owen, without turning up looking like a tramp. If clothes do indeed maketh the man, he wants to arrive looking the dog's bollocks, not the dog's breakfast.

Owen surveys the piles of discarded garments with a jaundiced eye and, cursing his stupidity, begins the laborious task of carefully folding and repacking his new wardrobe. Only now there seems to be a lot more to put back in than he took out. How could this be? It was a mystery. Like many a man before him, Owen had left his wife to do the packing and before his marriage had relied on his mother's expertise. Despite his lack of experience in these matters he struggles on manfully; and although he is forced more than once to empty the case and start all over again, he eventually gets some sort of system going and is well into packing the second suitcase when he realises that yet again, he has cocked up.

'Stupid. Stupid. Stupid!' Each cry is accompanied by a self-inflicted slap on the forehead. Owen angrily walks away from the bed, turns and comes back again. 'You should have sorted out what you're going to wear for the journey down first, shouldn't you, you stupid sod!' he shouts at the open mouth of the half packed suitcase.

He grabs a fistful of clothes and is about to turf them out onto the floor when calmer counsel prevails and he carefully removes the folded items and places them in piles; shirts in one, slacks in another and so on. When he has everything laid out on the bed once more, Owen takes time to review each pile of garments then, selecting a pair of light brown slacks, looks for something to go with them. An hour and several changes of clothes later, he stands in front of the mirror dressed in a tweed casual jacket, pale green shirt, light brown slacks and light tan, leather shoes. Owen smiles at his reflection, he is rather pleased with himself; Maureen couldn't have done a better job of dressing him. Who would have believed it? He looks quite the man about town. And they are a perfect fit. Another little bit of Sebastian's black magic.

It's early afternoon; the kids will soon be piling out of the school across the way and Owen still has the cases to re-pack. At this rate he won't be ready when Marlow returns with Sebastian to collect him. Failure is not an option, Owen reminds himself, and sets to with renewed determination.

*

Promptly at six, the Range Rover draws up at Owen's front gate. He watches it arrive from his bedroom window and runs downstairs. In the hallway, the suitcases stand ready and waiting with the garment bags draped over them. Marlow's highly polished shoes ring out on the pathway. Owen retreats to the lounge and waits for the bell to ring; it would be uncool to appear too eager and he is feeling particularly cool in his new clothes. The bell rings and Owen is leisurely in answering it.

'Good evening, sir. All set?'

'Yes, I'll just get my luggage.' He turns away from the door and reaches for one of the cases but the chauffeur is there before him.

'That's all right, sir, I'll take care of these. If you'd like to make your way to the car...' He waves a hand towards the front gate.

'Oh, right. Thank you.' In a moment the thin veneer of coolness Owen's been cultivating is peeled back to reveal his self-doubting, indecisive self. He has got it wrong again and they haven't left the house yet. 'Sorry,' he mumbles but continues to hover in the doorway.

'Is there something else, sir?'

Should he say this, 'Erm... could you make sure you shut the door properly when you've finished with the cases?'

The chauffeur is poker-faced. 'Don't you worry, sir, I'm quite used to shutting doors after people. I do it all the time.'

Of course he did. Oh God, he was never going to get the hang of this servant and master thing and certainly not over the course of this blasted weekend. They would see through him in an instant, despite the posh clothes.

With rather less aplomb than he came down the stairs with, Owen slopes off towards the waiting car. He hears footsteps behind him and before he can do it himself, Marlow opens the gate for him.

'After you, sir,' he says and steps aside to let him pass.

Sebastian, sat in the back of the car, is engrossed in something he has on his iPad. The tailgate door is open and the last rays of the dying sun fill the car's interior with a golden light. It's a striking image and the words of a hymn Owen sang as a schoolboy pop into his head; *"Bring me my bow of burning gold! Bring me my arrows of desire!"* How did the rest of it go? Something about *chariots of fire...* but he is unable to recall the exact line. No matter, the imagery conjured up by the poetry is a perfect description of Tantalus in this light. Then Marlow closes the tailgate and the moment is gone. The angel of light looks up from his iPad and is the envoy for the ruler of darkness once more.

Marlow comes round from the back of the car, opens the nearside rear door for him and Owen climbs in beside Sebastian. The Range-Rover's interior smells of leather and furniture polish overlaid with the spicy tang of Sebastian's cologne.

Tantalus puts the iPad down on the seat beside him and gives Owen an appraising look. 'My, but you have scrubbed up nicely,' he says.

'Thanks,' says Owen, flattered despite his nervousness regarding Sebastian's intentions towards him.

'Clothes maketh the man, eh.' Sebastian lifts a small section of the seat between them and produces two miniature bottles of whisky and two tumblers. 'This calls for a toast,' he says and, handing one of the glasses to Owen, pours them both a drink. 'Here's to a fresh start!' He clinks his glass against Owen's. 'This is where your journey really begins,' he says, beaming.

They drink. Marlow climbs in behind the wheel and starts the engine. Owen settles back into his seat and buckles up. The fiery liquor hits his stomach and begins spreading throughout his body, filling him with a warm sense of well-being. 'Where exactly are we going, or is this a magical mystery tour you're taking me on?'

'There's no mystery about it,' Sebastian assures him.

'We are spending the weekend in the Cotswolds at Sir Freddy Lomax's country retreat, *Crackmans*. Do you know it?' Owen shakes his head. 'No? Wait till you see it, Owen. Bea-u-tiful place, he's rolling in it –I mean, he's totally, unbelievably, filthy, stinking rich!'

Sir Freddy sounds intimidatingly successful and Owen spends the rest of the journey worrying about his social skills, or lack of them, and how on earth he could ever have hoped to hide the fact that he is a fraud; a changeling.

*

Sebastian hadn't exaggerated. Crackmans Hall is a fine example of 18th century opulence. Set in acres of parkland, it's Vanburgh and Capability Brown; the kind of house Owen has only ever visited when National Trusting with Maureen. As they sweep up the winding driveway in the darkness they catch glimpses of the floodlit house between gaps in the parkland's trees. The driveway is so long that in daylight the house would not be visible from the road. Sir Freddy Lomax is obviously a man who values his privacy, Owen decides. Earlier at the main gate a tuxedoed 'heavy' had waved them down. As they came to a halt, another 'heavy' stepped out from the shadows of the Lodge House doorway clutching a clip-board, and approached the driver's window. Marlow obligingly lowered it and the thick-set man leaned in; his well-developed biceps bulging beneath his dinner jacket. He peered at each of them in turn then demanded to see their invitations. Marlow handed them over and the man consulted his list. Satisfied that they were in fact bona fide guests, he returned the invitations to the chauffeur and signalled to his colleague to open the gate.

'Welcome to Crackmans Hall, gentlemen. Enjoy your stay,' he'd said and stepped away from the car as another vehicle announced its arrival with the glare of headlights and a tooting horn.

The Range Rover's headlamps splash cold white light across the front elevation of the house which is dominated by an impressive four-column Ionic portico. Curving down on both sides of it there is an elegant stone staircase. Leaving the engine running, Marlow holds the door open for each of them in turn then, getting into the car, takes it back round to the side of the house, presumably to the servant's entrance.

Awestruck, Owen stares up at the massive stone edifice. He can't believe that all this belongs to one man; how had Lomax managed to amass the kind of money needed to buy a palace like this? The Lodge alone must be worth two or three times more than his brother had paid for his new house. Brushing a hand through his hair Owen realises that he is trembling. The air temperature is noticeably lower than when he left home but that's not why he is shaking.

Sir Freddy Lomax is a big man in every sense of the word; standing over six feet tall, he is built like a rugby forward and has piercing blue eyes that look out on the world from beneath a mane of dark blond hair.

Owen had hung back when Sebastian had started up the stone staircase, not wanting to be the first in line when they entered the hedge fund millionaire's baronial home. Now, as he waits nervously to exchange handshakes with his host, he is wishing he'd made a run for it whilst

Sebastian's back was turned.

'And this must be Mr Leadbeater.'

This comes not from the great man but his Lady wife; a small woman in comparison to her husband but still tall for a woman. She comes from a titled family – old money – but by the time Lomax came courting, the money had gone and all they had was their title and the crumbling pile that had been Crackmans Hall, before Lomax's new money had restored it to its former glory.

Jemima Lomax looks every inch the Lady in an elegant full-length evening dress; her auburn hair swept up behind her head is held in place with a diamond studded clasp. Matching diamond droppers dangle from her ears and a diamond choker glitters at her slim, white throat.

'Good evening, your Ladyship,' says Owen tremulously. There's a moment's awkward silence and he senses that he has committed some breach of etiquette, but can't think what it could be. Should he have kissed her hand rather than shaken it? Perhaps he should have bowed?

Lomax chuckles; a deep rumble that sets his jowls quivering, 'We don't stand on ceremony here, Owen,' he assures him with a slap on the shoulder. 'It's Freddy and Jemima to you. You're here to relax and enjoy yourself. We'll talk some more later. Until dinner then. Robinson here will show you to your rooms.'

A small wiry man appears unbidden at Lady Jemima's side. He wears a green uniform and looks like he just stepped out of a BBC costume drama. 'This way, gentlemen,' he says.

They leave the splendour of the vestibule with its Italian marble floor and the Trompe l'oeil frescoes behind as they ascend the right-hand staircase – the staircase here mirrors the one outside – and on up to the first floor.

'You're in your usual room, Mr Tantalus,' he says over his shoulder. They process along a corridor whose walls are hung with priceless works of art and down a further corridor where Robinson stops outside the first door they come to. He opens the door for Sebastian then turns to Owen, 'And you're just next door, Mr Leadbeater.'

'Cosy,' says Sebastian and manages to convey a whole other world of meaning in that one word.

Colouring, Owen hurriedly follows Robinson into one of the most luxurious bedrooms he has ever been in, even when visiting National Trust properties. The room is dominated by a huge four-poster bed with a carved canopy and hung with rich red and gold patterned drapes. He idly wonders if all the rooms are kitted out with a four poster; for many it is an erotic fantasy to make love in one – himself included. The walls and floor are panelled and boarded in the same dark oak as the bed, with a large patterned rug to break up the lines and provide a splash of colour. To Owen's untrained eye all the furniture in the room appears to be antique and the soft furnishings the best that money can buy. This is living on a grand scale, thinks Owen; multiply the money spent in this one room by the number of rooms in the house and furnishing Crackmans Hall must have cost a king's ransom. Still, judging by what he'd seen and heard of the man so far, it wouldn't have made much of a dent in Lomax's huge fortune.

His suitcase has been placed on the bed and his clothes laid out for him. As Owen begins to change for dinner, he realises he still has very little notion of what a hedge fund is. He is still struggling to tie his bow tie – a proper one, not the kind attached to a piece of elastic that he is used to – when Sebastian knocks on the door and entering, announces it's time to go down to dinner.

'Here, let me do that for you,' he says, as Owen tries for the umpteenth time to tie the damned thing. 'Tying a bow tie is an art that most men fail to master. They usually leave it to their wives – not an option in your case of course – luckily for you, I am a master of the art… voilà,' he says with a flourish and it's done.

Sebastian may be an angel from the dark side and an irritating know-it-all, but Owen is grateful to have someone to walk down with, as the thought of entering a roomful of people terrifies him. Even so, he won't know anybody and he possesses all the social skills of a hermit. What on earth could a world-class loser like him have to say that would be of any interest to a bunch of toffs and high flyers? Small talk it was called, but it was no small thing for Owen. These people lived on a different planet from those like him who have had to settle for a life that is only one step above mere existence. Owen is still mulling over the problem of what to say when they arrive downstairs.

Aperitifs are being served in the drawing room. Freddy Lomax lounges against a grand piano; drink in hand, he is talking animatedly with a well-known rock star; famous, or more accurately infamous, for his excesses. He is more likely to appear on the front pages of the red tops than on stage these days.

Her back to an Adam fireplace, Jemima Lomax holds court with a group of women and an up-and-coming young male fashion designer who, defying convention, wears an outfit which combines top hat and tails with the colourful ribbons and bows of a troubadour. Amongst the women Owen recognises another face from the tabloids; a beautiful fashion model with a dazzling career and a troubled private life. She appears to find everything her hostess says incredibly funny and Owen suspects she is either drunk or high on something. Elsewhere he spots an actor he has seen on TV many times over the years, but can never put a name to; always in supporting roles, he never gets to play the leading man. Owen, who has some experience of playing out a life in someone else's shadow, knows just how that feels.

A young woman dressed in a crisp white blouse with a black bow tie, pencil slim black skirt and heels approaches the pair, and offers them a drink from the tray she is holding. They each take one, but as his companion raises the glass to his lips, somebody shouts, 'Oh look, it's Sebastian,' and they are immediately surrounded by a noisy group of people eager to have a word with him. His acolytes pull Sebastian away to a quiet corner and huddle round him, leaving Owen on his own in the middle of the room. This is precisely the situation Owen was anxious to avoid and suddenly he feels isolated and vulnerable; it's as if his clothes have been ripped off him and everyone is staring at his naked body. The model is laughing again but now Owen thinks her laughter is aimed at him. He stands there stiffly like a mannequin in a shop window display in his ridiculous tux and clutching his only prop – the glass of vermouth. He wonders if he should join one of the various groups dotted about the room, but which one to approach first? What if they cold shoulder him? He pictures himself moving from one to another and being rejected by them all.

He is rescued from further embarrassment by his hostess, who gathers everyone up and ushers them into the dining room. The lighting in here is subdued, creating a feeling of intimacy that a room this size wouldn't have in brighter light, but the splendour of the riches on display remain undimmed. Running almost the full length of the room is a huge dining table that can seat up to thirty people. Georgian silverware glistens in the candlelight and from the walls Jemima's ancestors gaze down disapprovingly at their *nouveau riche* usurpers.

Owen scrutinises the place cards for his name and discovers he has been seated well below the salt; joining those lesser mortals who have yet to rise to the giddy heights occupied by the Lomax's and their favoured guests. Chief among these is Sebastian Tantalus who sits at Sir Freddie's right hand, which would explain the financier's irresistible rise and rise, thinks Owen. This sets him wondering just how many of those seated at Lomax's table also owe their success to a leg-up from his mentor. A cursory glance at the other end of the table is enough to convince Owen that more than half the people here are in hock to the soul trader.

All heads turn in his direction as Sebastian begins laughing like a hyena at something the rock star has just said.

'He's a friend of yours, isn't he?' The speaker is a pasty-faced man a little younger than Owen. Balding and overweight, he leans across the table and peers at Owen over a pair of rimless bi-focals. 'I saw you walk in with him earlier on.'

'He's not what I would call a friend… ' says Owen guardedly, 'More of a mentor really. He's, er, helping me choose a new career.' He wonders how much the man knows about Sebastian and if he will buy this benign description of the dark angel's activities.

'Really? That's interesting. I'm looking to change direction myself,' the man says, with an eagerness that runs close to desperation. 'Do you think you could introduce me to your friend?'

Oh, you will be easy meat for Sebastian, thinks Owen, and is tempted to warn him off, but he can see this would be futile; the man is very obviously teetering on the brink of some great calamity and will approach Tantalus himself, if Owen doesn't make the introduction for him.

'Sure, why not,' concedes Owen, though he doubts he is doing the poor man a favour.

The man pulls out a leather card wallet and, after a great deal of fumbling, manages to extract one of his business cards. 'My card,' he says and hands it to Owen.

Owen examines it; Daniel Poulter, financial director, he reads… and wonders what kind of trouble he is in. In all probability it involves money and it isn't too big a stretch, given his occupation, to assume that the man has been stealing from his employers. He looks up from the card and back at Poulter; at the perspiration beading his upper lip, the dark shadows ringing his eyes, and is almost certain of it.

'I'll see that Sebastian gets it,' he tells him and pockets the card.

'Oh, thank you Mister… I'm so sorry, I'm afraid I didn't catch your name.'

'Owen, Owen Leadbeater.'

'Pleased to meet you, Owen,' says Poulter effusively, 'I owe you one,' and for a moment he looks ten years younger. Desperate Dan, thinks Owen; the poor sod doesn't know what he is letting himself in for...

The meal drags on, course after course; each accompanied by the appropriate wines, until Owen is so full he feels his stomach must burst. Conversation is just as slow as Owen's companions have about as much to say for themselves as he does. It's far livelier at the other end of the table and Owen is relieved when the final course having been served and consumed, the gentlemen are invited to take their coffee in the billiard room. When Owen gets up out of his seat he finds his head is as light as his stomach is heavy; weeble-like he momentarily wobbles but does not fall; the extra ballast he is carrying ensuring that he stays upright. Feeling decidedly queasy he takes the ever present Robinson to one side and asks the way to the nearest bathroom.

'Follow me, sir,' he says, and leads Owen back into the room where they had gathered for pre-dinner drinks. Long hair dangling over the keyboard, the rock star is slumped over the grand. His right hand hovers just above the keys, fingers silently miming a melody that only he can hear. Owen has heard of air guitar but air piano?

'Hey, Man,' the rock star says without looking up, as they pass through and into the hallway.

'It's just down there on the left,' Robinson says, pointing to a door let into the oak panelled walls.

Owen thanks him and, the bitter taste of bile filling his mouth, hurries down the corridor. At the door he pauses, having realised he has no idea which way to go after he has finished here, but Robinson has anticipated his next question.

'You'll find the billiard room at the end of the hallway, sir,' he says obligingly.

Owen is about to thank him again but quickly clamps his mouth shut as he begins to heave. Wrenching the door open, he dives inside and falling to his knees, he is violently and spectacularly sick. It pours out of him with the force of an Icelandic geyser, spattering walls, floor and finally, the front of Owen's tuxedo. He stares aghast at the mess he has made; watches in horrified fascination as solid goblets of the stuff go sliding down the wall. Before he can do anything about it, he is being sick again and continues to retch long after his stomach is empty; dry heaves that strain muscle and tear soft tissue.

Owen is still on his knees as if in prayer, when there is a genteel cough behind him. He brings his head up and grabbing some toilet tissue, wipes the vomit from his chin. Robinson stands in the doorway, his face an impassive mask. The man must be utterly appalled by Owen's behaviour and the mess he has made and yet, it's as if he doesn't see it. The servant's equanimity, his sang-froid is remarkable.

'Mr Robinson, I'm so sorry,' says a wretched Owen. 'If you fetch me a mop, I'll clean this mess up.'

'It's just Robinson, sir, and don't worry, I'll see to it. But first I think we should get you up to your room. Come along sir.'

Owen tries to push himself up off the floor but all that retching seems to have sapped him of his strength. Fortunately, the unflappable Robinson is at hand and the diminutive manservant is a lot stronger than he looks. He hauls Owen to his feet and then, whipping out a walkie-talkie, arranges for someone to come and clean up the mess. After first checking that the corridor is clear of guests, he escorts Owen up to his room by way of a back staircase used only by the servants.

Now that Robinson has gone, taking Owen's soiled tuxedo with him to be sponged and cleaned, Owen has time to appreciate the true enormity of the social embarrassment that has been averted, thanks to the manservant's intervention. With a speed and efficiency that he would not have believed possible, all evidence of his shameful behaviour has been expunged. How much easier his life would be, Owen muses, if only he had the means to employ a Robinson of his own. He takes a last look round at his luxurious surroundings before turning off the bedside lamp; this a lifestyle I could easily get used to, he decides, as he slides deeper under the covers.

Owen sleeps the sleep of the dead. As he slowly drifts up through the layers of wakefulness, he is dimly aware of the pop, pop, pop, of the shooters as they go about their murderous business, but doesn't immediately identify it as such. It's only when he squints at his watch that he realises how late it is; he has slept through breakfast and will miss the shoot. This does not unduly trouble him as he is not yet ready to eat anything, and has never understood the pleasure the rich and titled take in killing defenceless birds and animals. They called it sport, but that implied that the hunted had a reasonable chance of surviving.

When Owen throws back the bedcovers and sits up, his chest and abdomen are painfully sore; it's as if someone has put a hand down his throat whilst he slept and pulled his guts out. He lingers under the shower before shaving and, selecting something casual and sporty from the wardrobe Sebastian has provided him with, makes his way downstairs.

The house appears to be deserted and in the cavernous hallway, the returning echo of his footsteps the only sounds of life. Owen wanders from room to room and finding all of them unoccupied, returns to the hall. He is about to slip back upstairs when Robinson appears on the landing above him.

'Ah, there you are Mr Leadbeater, I've just been looking for you. Mr Tantalus sends his compliments, sir, and invites you to join him and the rest of the guests for lunch. You'll find them down by the lake.'

Owen approaches the lake with some trepidation – he is the odd one out again – turning up late and explanations will have to be made. Keep it simple he tells himself; no need to go into too much detail. He wonders how much of the sorry story Robinson has relayed to Sebastian. As the manservant was leaving his room last night, Owen had asked him to let Mr Tantalus know that he was feeling unwell and would not be joining the gentlemen in the billiard room. He hopes the little man was discreet.

There are shouts of 'here he is,' as Owen comes into sight. He puts on a brave smile and waves. The scene resembles an impressionist painting; Lomax and his guests sit or sprawl on large tartan rugs strung out like a series of islands in the shade of some ancient willows. They are helping themselves to food and drink from vast wicker hampers. Behind them the lake sparkles and shimmers like a mirage in the afternoon sun.

'Come and sit here,' says Lady Jemima, patting a vacant space beside her.

As he weaves his way through the archipelago of rugs, Owen scrutinises each of the upturned faces looking for signs that they know more about last night's events than they are letting on, but learns only that most of them have no idea who the latecomer is. He squats down between Sebastian and Lady Jemima and she hands him a glass of champagne.

'Kind of you to join us,' says Sebastian. His tone is pleasant enough, but when Owen's gaze meets Sebastian's, those dark eyes flash their disapproval.

'Yes, where have you been?' chimes Lady Jemima. 'We've missed you.' In the diffused sunlight filtering through the willow's foliage, her auburn hair is the colour of burnished copper.

'Tummy upset,' Owen explains.

'Well, I hope it wasn't something you've eaten here,' says Sir Freddy indignantly from the other side of his wife. 'We rather pride ourselves on the standard of the cuisine at Crackmans Hall.'

'Don't worry, Freddy, Owen's something of a martyr to his digestive system, aren't you Owen?' And Sebastian gives Owen's shoulder a spiteful squeeze. The pain is sharp but brief; like having a large bird of prey land on his shoulder and take off again.

'Yes, it runs in the family.' They all laugh and Owen is at a loss to understand why.

'Runs, d'ya see? You said, runs in the family,' explains Sir Freddy, and they all laugh again.

Owen colours; why hadn't he seen that one coming before he opened his mouth? Owen's discomfort increases as the joke is relayed from island to island, like a stone skipping across a pond and, just as that stone will inevitably sink, so his spirits plunge.

'And how's your appetite today, Owen?' Lady Jemima enquires, holding up a plate, 'Can I tempt you to something?'

Owen doesn't really want anything but makes a small selection from the hamper out of politeness to his hostess. As he picks at a cold leg of roast chicken, he chews over his latest gaff and how, despite Robinson's valiant efforts on his behalf, he became his own informer and blew the whistle on himself. Owen is still picking at his own flesh when he hears a splash behind him and, whirling round, sees that some fool has jumped fully clothed into the lake. Others follow his example; most of them stripping down to their underwear, but a sizeable number throw off all their clothes and jump in naked.

Owen is alarmed when, without warning, Sebastian jumps to his feet and, shielding his eyes, stares towards the lake. Owen has no desire to go swimming, fully clothed or otherwise, and hopes Sebastian won't insist on it as a way of punishing him for his non-attendance in the billiard room last night and at this morning's shoot. For the moment Sebastian is engrossed; his eyes following every move of the frolicking bathers then, his lips curling into a lascivious smile, he begins to unbutton his shirt.

'Oh, look out, he's going in!' says Sir Freddy with a throaty chuckle. 'What about you Owen, d'ya fancy a dip?'

Not on your life, thinks Owen; Sebastian has that familiar glint in his eye and there was no knowing what kind of hell he was bent on. 'Ummm…' Owen replies noncommittally.

'In that case, let me show you around the estate,' says Lomax before Owen is obliged to make a decision either way. 'That alright with you, Sebastian?'

Sebastian is down to his Calvin Klein's, 'What?' he says, his mind clearly on other things.

'That's settled then.' says Sir Freddy. He turns to his wife and gives her a peck on the cheek. 'What about you, Jemima?'

'I'm perfectly happy where I am, thank you,' she says, casting an approving eye over Sebastian's perfect physique.

Later Owen will wonder if the whole thing was pre-arranged, but for now it feels like he is being invited to become a member of a very select club.

'Give me a hand here, will you, Owen?' says Sir Freddy who is struggling to raise his huge bulk.

Owen helps his host to his feet and Sir Freddy brushes himself down. They step out from under the willows and into the bright sunlight. Blinking in the sudden glare, Owen stares out across the parkland and begins to appreciate just what he has let himself in for. There is an awful lot of it and it's a very warm day to embark on a grand tour.

As they walk away from the lake, Owen looks back over his shoulder in time to see Lady Jemima step out of her dress. He can't tell if anyone is with her and in any case, it's none of his business what Sir Freddy's wife gets up to when her husband's back is turned. The man himself seems unconcerned; right now he is on his mobile phone, asking someone up at the house to bring the cart round.

Owen was expecting a horse and trap, but what arrives minutes later is one of those electric golf carts that

American golfers, in particular, use to travel between holes. At the wheel is the little manservant Robinson looking as inscrutable as ever. The cart comes to a halt and Robinson steps out. Nodding to them both, he makes his way back to the house.

Squeezing in behind the wheel, Lomax invites Owen to 'hop aboard.' The cart is a two-seater; a bench seat with individual back rests, and there is not much room left for Owen. They set off at the leisurely pace dictated by the cart's electric motor; Sir Freddy pointing out features of particular significance or interest.

First stop is the stable block where Sir Freddy keeps a collection of classic cars rather than a string of horses. Gleaming paintwork and shiny bright chrome have replaced the glossy flanks and gleaming mane, but there is horsepower here and lots of it, for they are all sports cars. Lomax walks Owen around each one; sounding like Jeremy Clarkson as he rattles off details of their specification and performance; engine capacity, brake-horsepower, gear ratios – most of which goes over non-driver Owen's head. When he squeezes himself into the driver's seat of a 1953 MG Midget, Owen wonders why Lomax buys these cars; how a man as big as he is gets into them, let alone drives them.

Their journey ends in the deer park. Lomax pulls over onto the grass and leaning back in his seat, lights up a Churchill-sized cigar. The two men sit in silence for a while and watch a herd of red deer peacefully grazing in the late afternoon sunshine. The grassy acres stretch away to the horizon; the green graduating to blue, transmuted by the distance. Owen is the first to break the silence, 'It's hard to imagine anyone owning a place like this.'

Sir Freddy smiles, 'I don't, not really... I mean, I bought the place right enough, but it's been in Jemima's family for generations. I may have the money, but they have the history. Nothing tops that. Class, d'ya see... it's like love. You can't buy it.' He puffs out a great cloud of blue smoke. 'Still, it's not a bad result for an East End boy.' He looks pleased to see the surprise on Owen's face. 'Oh yearse, I talk proper nah,' he says, adopting a mockney drawl, 'A posh accent is something money *can* buy.' He chuckles at the memory. 'So, what about you, Owen, what are you going do when you grow up, eh?'

'Depends... ' Owen hesitates to go further; whilst he strongly suspects that Sir Freddy has been signed up by Sebastian, he can't be certain; and he has no desire to get any blacker in Sebastian's bad books.

'No need to be coy, Owen. We both know why you're here.' He throws his arms wide. 'I didn't get where I am today without a little help from our mutual friend. So, I'm going to tell you a little story,' he rolls his cigar between his fingers, 'listen carefully and you may learn something to your advantage, as they say...'

*

Later, in his room as he changes for dinner, there is a light tap on his door, and Sebastian walks straight in on him.

'Ah, the wanderer has returned,' he says and, leaning against one of the ornately carved bedposts, folds his arms. 'You're proving very elusive this weekend, Owen, what have you been up to, I wonder?' He studies Owen's face intently as if the answer may be written there. 'Well, have you made any useful contacts while you've been here?

'I was talking to a guy last night who seemed very keen to meet you.' He retrieves Poulter's business card from the bedside table and hands it to Tantalus. 'You'll have no trouble signing him up, he seemed quite desperate. Is there some commission in it for me if you do?'

Sebastian snorts. 'Don't push your luck, Owen. You haven't exactly covered yourself in glory this weekend.' Sebastian slips the card into the back pocket of his trousers. 'Oh, by the way, you won't be needing the monkey suit; it's casual wear tonight, or fancy dress if you prefer. Personally I find this fetish the rich have for dressing up a little tedious, but if you want to, I believe costumes are available for those who haven't brought one with them. Anyway, it's up to you. I'll see you downstairs.'

Owen isn't remotely interested in donning a costume; he had managed to look like a clown without even dressing up, the night they had gone to *The Pussy Galore Club*. But that was the old Owen, he reminds himself; he has a new wardrobe now and he will look good in whatever he decides to put on.

When he joins the others in 'The Music Room', Sebastian's doleful prediction about the rich and their fetish for 'dressing up' proves all too correct. The room is populated by Marie Antoinette, Julius Caesar and dozens of other historical figures, many of which Owen has difficulty in identifying. Sir Freddy is holding court as *The Phantom of the Opera*, whilst his wife has opted for a *Cat Woman* costume. Owen is surprised and somewhat alarmed to see that many of those who have chosen to wear a costume along with many of those who haven't, are wearing masks instead. On its own it would be nothing but there is a sexual tension in the air this evening which the masks serve only to increase.

As Owen makes his way into the dining room, a tubby figure sidles up to him. Owen recognises him immediately despite the full length wig and frock coat; it's Poulter.

'Did you mention me to your friend?' he asks.

'Yep, he's got your card. Sebastian's a busy man, but I'm sure he'll be in touch before too long.'

Poulter grabs Owen's hand and shakes it vigorously. 'Thanks, thanks very much. You're a pal.'

I'm not, thinks Owen. I'm so not…

The meal that follows is a much simpler affair than the previous evening with just three courses; little more than a light supper by comparison.

Shortly afterwards the company retire to a large, ornate drawing room which is dominated by a huge crystal chandelier. A long table has been set up at one end of the room which is laden with bottles of wine and spirits of every kind. Champagne is served and then the servants leave the guests to serve themselves. Someone lowers the lights, puts on some music; "That old black magic," Sinatra croons silkily, and people begin to dance. Moments later, a door opens and a plump, blonde-haired woman in her fifties enters the room. She is naked but for a black choker with a pearl dropper hanging from it and the smile she is wearing. She works her way around the room, embracing each of the men in turn, and some of the women. Then kissing them on the mouth she removes a jacket here, unzips a dress there. As she moves on, the recipients of her kisses remove the rest of their clothing and, having done so, help those nearest them off with theirs. Before long everyone in the room is naked; everyone but Owen and Sebastian, who looks on with a joyful smile on his face.

He turns to Owen standing at his side, an untouched glass of champagne in his hand. 'Come on, Owen, get your kit off,' he says encouragingly.

'You must be joking,' Owen replies. He can't believe his eyes. This was the last thing he was expecting to happen. The sedate politeness on display at dinner had given no inkling of what was to follow.

'That wasn't a request, Owen. It was an order. You need all the practice you can get if we're ever to get lust out of the way before you grow too old to get it up anymore.' He pushes Owen into the melange of naked flesh. 'Go on, fill your boots!'

By a horrible coincidence Sebastian's shove throws Owen into the path of the blonde with the choker whose surprise appearance sparked off this orgy of abandonment.

'Oh darling,' she giggles shrilly. 'You're keen.' She throws a pudgy arm around his neck, 'Oooh, is that for me dear,' she says, and taking the glass of Champagne from him, drains it in one go. Carelessly tossing the empty flute over her shoulder, she forcefully presses her wet lips against his and attempts to unzip his trouser fly. Owen tries to push her away, but a cavorting couple come blundering into them, and they are sent sprawling onto the floor. Landing heavily on his back with the hefty blonde on top of him leaves Owen struggling for breath. As he writhes in agony beneath her, she mistakes his frenzied panting for an urgent desire to possess her and, encouraged by a laughing Sebastian, begins tearing at his clothes.

When Owen recovers, it's to find he is hopelessly entangled amidst a group of writhing, naked couples; men with women; women with women and men, *mano a mano* – Sebastian amongst them. All around him couples are moaning and groaning like animals. It's disgusting and at the same time, irresistibly arousing. The pudgy blonde in the choker is astride him; rising and falling on him with increasingly rapid strokes. Her large, droopy breasts flop up and down with a sound like a wet slap. Owen closes his eyes, thinks about another blonde who once upon a time sang happy birthday to the charismatic ruler of the new Camelot.

Part Two

Redemption

5: BESIDE THE SEASIDE, BESIDE THE SEA

Owen stares at the young woman who stands at the window. Viewed in this light she looks far lovelier than he remembers her being at the *Pussy Galore Club*. At the same time she seems a lot more ordinary – it's the clothes that make her look less exotic, he decides. Unaware that she is being watched, Avril gazes out disconsolately through the rain spattered glass at the lowering clouds and the deserted beach; the rumble of the surf reduced to a soft murmur by the double-glazing.

The stormy weather provides the mood music for the way things have been going since Owen arrived some five weeks ago. The house that Sebastian has rented is one of a row of almost identical properties which line the seafront, all of them holiday lets or B & Bs. At Sebastian's behest, Owen has been pursuing a woman of the town. Her name is Agnes Rushworth and she runs a Christian bookshop. She is the chosen one. Not in *The Matrix* sense of being some sort of messiah but as the victim of one of the soul trader's diabolical schemes. Owen's task is to seduce – corrupt her would be a more accurate term – it's a dirty game and Owen's heart isn't in it, which is why Sebastian has summoned Avril down here to harden his resolve, as it were.

Owen drags himself off the bed to join her. 'Still raining,' he says. It's stating the obvious but he can't think of anything else to say. For several days now they have been forced to stay indoors as violent winds and torrential rain lash this small Welsh seaside town. He long ago exhausted his limited repertoire of conversation starters. Spotting a large bird on the cliffs that dominate the north end of the beach he says, 'You know, I think that's an albatross perched on that cliff.'

Avril's gaze follows the line of his pointing finger. 'I don't think so,' she says dismissively.

'Why not?'

'Because, they spend most of their lives on the wing,' she tells him.

'Perhaps this one's knackered. Must be tiring, flapping their wings all the time.' He knows he is talking nonsense but anything's better than the long silence that preceded it.

Avril gives him a scornful look. 'They glide.'

'Could be injured…'

'They live in the South Atlantic?' A shriller tone reflects her irritation but Owen blunders on; the needle stuck in the groove.

'What, all of the time?'

'Most of it, yes.'

Owen dredges his memory for the one fact he has stored away about the birds. 'They're supposed to be bad luck, aren't they?'

'Only if you kill one and you happen to be a superstitious sailor.'

'Oh right. You seem to know a lot about them.'

'I saw a documentary once,' she says, her eyes fixed on some faraway horizon.

'Must have missed that one. I love those Richard Attenborough nature programs, don't you?'

'David. It's David Attenborough. Richard's the film director.'

'You're not just a pretty face, are you?'

A glimmer of a smile briefly crosses Avril's lips. 'I put on the dumb blonde act for the punters. Most of them are brain-dead anyway. They feel more comfortable with a bimbo.'

Owen hopes she doesn't think of him like that. He has grown rather fond of her company; too fond, too dependent, he realises. Her arrival three days ago has been the one bright spot in an otherwise gloomy period for him and he's clung to her with a puppy-like devotion ever since.

'I can imagine. I don't know, what's it all about, eh?' he says

'What?'

'Life,' he says with a sigh. 'You're born. Life's a bitch...'

'And then you die,' Avril says in unison. She smiles then, suddenly serious, 'Yours is going to end a whole lot sooner, you know, if you don't hurry up and nail that bible-basher. It's been five weeks, Sebastian won't wait much longer.'

'I know, I know,' he says and turning back into the

room, clasps his hands behind his head. He stands there for a moment, head thrown back staring at the ceiling, then turns to face her and his hands fall to his side. 'Oh why did Sebastian have to choose her?' he groans.

'I've no idea,' she says tiredly. 'And frankly, I don't care. I just want to get out of this dump and get back to my son. So please, just do the business with – what's her name again?'

'Agnes.'

'Agnes?' Her mouth turns down in a grimace. 'What *were* her parents thinking of, saddling their daughter with an old fashioned name like that?'

'She *is* an old fashioned girl. Huh, I say girl, she's not much younger than me.'

'Well, that's what you wanted, isn't it? Someone nearer your own age.'

'It's not that.'

'What then?'

'She's just so… well, NICE!'

With a sigh Avril comes away from the window and its desolate view, and throwing an arm around Owen's neck, places a warm peck on his cheek. She moves her mouth down and he can feel her breath on his ear. 'Owen, that's so lovely,' she coos sweetly. 'She's nice. You're nice. It's a marriage made in heaven.' Then harshly, 'Now, bloody well get on with it!'

She pushes past him, heading for the door, but Owen grabs her by the arm and pulls her back. 'I can't do it, Avril, don't you see? She's *too* nice,' he says. 'That's the problem.'

Avril pulls his hand away and straightens her sweater. 'No, Owen. Your problem is you're afraid of women,' she says hotly.

Exasperated, Owen throws his hands up in the air. 'Oh, so now you're a psychiatrist! Where's that little pearl of wisdom from; the lap dancer's guide to psycho-analysis or did you watch a documentary?'

Avril folds her arms across her chest. 'No, Southampton,' she says with an icy coolness.

'Southampton... what's Southampton got to do with it?'

'Southampton University, it's where I got my degree in psychology. What's more, I've got the graduation photo and certificate to prove it.'

'And are you wearing a 'G' string with your mortarboard or a gown?'

'Mortarboard, gown, and diploma,' she says proudly. '*The Full Monty.*'

Owen digests this revelation for a moment. It doesn't sit easily with the image he has put together of Avril and her chosen profession. 'If you're so clever, how come you're wriggling around on men's laps for a living?'

'I got the degree. I just didn't get the job that goes with it,' she says defensively.

'I see. If you can't use your brain, wiggle your arse, is that it? Well you're not the first pretty girl to earn a living doing that, I suppose.'

Avril unfolds her arms and places them on her hips. 'At least I got off my arse and got myself a job!' she says, jabbing a finger into his chest.

'Oh, I wondered when you'd get round to that. Well, I prefer to keep my clothes on when I'm working, thank you.'

'That's because no one would pay *you* to take them

off!' Another stab with her finger and Owen backs away, but Avril comes after him.

'But that's not all they pay you for, though, is it?' he counters.

'Oh, you bastard!' she says her face contorted by her anger and gives him a two handed shove.

Owen is backed up against the window now and, with nowhere to go, he raises his hands in surrender. 'Okay. Okay. That was a cheap shot. I'm sorry.'

'You had better be.'

'So, what do I call you then, Doctor Avril?'

'It's still Avril, if you're going to be nice and stop taking your frustrations out on me. It's not my fault your life is in a mess.'

'Yours on the other hand is hunky-dory, of course,' he says, scathingly.

'Obviously not, or I wouldn't have signed up for this wet weekend in hell.' Her eyes glisten as though she is about to cry. She turns away from him and, crossing to the bed, perches on the edge of it. She looks so sorrowful and Owen wonders if she is missing her son; who's looking after the boy while his mother's here babysitting him.

Owen sits down on the bed beside her. 'This isn't hell,' he says quietly. 'Hell is feeling alone even when you're with someone.'

'Maureen?'

'Yes, Maureen.'

And he tells her how he and Maureen met while they were still teenagers. How he fell for the shy 17 year old with the cornflower blue eyes and the mousey hair. She was as quiet as a mouse too; to begin with anyway. Their long courtship and the celibacy that Maureen insisted on because she said she wanted to be a virgin bride. A stance he respected but found hard to endure as his own hormones raged and his desires remained unsatisfied. Even after they had become engaged, Maureen was still reluctant to name the day – the signs were there from early on but he'd been too blind to see them; misinterpreted them as symptomatic of her innate shyness. The marriage brought some release from his longings but their love-making was always a desperate affair in which Maureen played little part and seemed to take scant pleasure in. There followed years of rows and recriminations until finally, too exhausted to argue any more, they had settled for silence.

'Sounds bleak,' says Avril, when Owen drifts off into a long contemplative silence of his own.

'As I said, it was hell.'

Owen slowly gets to his feet, and drifting over to the window, stares out towards the horizon with unfocussed eyes. Cloaked in mist and rain it's hard to tell where the sea ends and the sky begins. 'Does it really exist, do you think? Hell, I mean. Only I've never really believed in either place myself,' he says.

'Sebastian's proof of that, surely. And if hell exists, then heaven must too. In which case we may have made a bad bargain, don't you think?'

Owen's head swivels sharply in Avril's direction, 'Is he though?' he says, suddenly animated. 'We've only got his word for it. He could just as easily be an alien nasty from a more advanced civilisation.' A further idea occurs to him. 'His crew mates could have mutinied and marooned him here. Yes, that's it, and now he gets his jollies messing with the minds of us primitive earthlings.'

Avril struggles to keep a straight face. 'You are joking, right? Sebastian is ET's twisted cousin?'

'Why not, is it any crazier than believing he's a little red demon from hell? Most scientists believe there's intelligent life out there somewhere.' He waves a hand at the rain splashed window.

'In a galaxy far, far away, no doubt.' Avril shakes her head. 'I think you must have cabin fever.' She gets to her feet. 'And the best cure for that is a breath of fresh air. Come on you, let's go for a walk.'

Owen shrugs his shoulders and smiles, as if he doesn't quite believe what he is saying, either. He glances through the window. On the beach a middle-aged woman in a woolly hat throws a ball for her dog. Barking excitedly, the Labrador scampers off after it, paws kicking up great clumps of wet sand. 'Yeah, why not. Looks like it's stopped raining at last. But don't think this lets you off the hook.'

'What do you mean?'

'I mean, it's your turn to spill the beans. I've told you why I signed up with Sebastian. What's your story?'

'The usual tale of desperation, nothing very interesting,' she says guardedly.

'Oh, I see, the lap dancer's answer to Sigmund Freud will bare her arse but not her soul.'

A frown furrows Avril's brow. 'Don't start that again. I just don't want to talk about it, that's all.'

'You don't want to talk to anybody or just me in particular?'

'I hardly know you.'

'I thought that was the whole point of counselling, unburdening yourself to a stranger?'

'You're not exactly a stranger either.'

Owen colours as he recalls the night she went down on him and her dark hair spilled into his lap. He wants to run his fingers through those dark strands now, but he resists the temptation 'And you're just playing with words to avoid…'

But Avril interrupts him, 'Leave it Owen, please. Just leave it. You don't know what you're getting yourself into here.'

'I confided in you.'

'How old are you, Owen? This isn't a case of you show me yours and I'll show you mine. I didn't ask you to tell me your story, you chose to tell me. I didn't bully you into it.'

'I'm sorry, I didn't mean to pry. Oh God,' he says as a tear runs down her cheek. Owen hurriedly fumbles in his pocket for a handkerchief and hands it to her.

Avril takes it from him and dabs at her eyes. 'Thanks,' she says, handing it back. 'Look, don't take it personally. I just don't know you well enough yet, that's all. Right now what I really need is a hug.' She gives him a wan smile. 'Just a hug, mind you.'

Owen folds his arms around her and pulls her close. The difference in their respective height means that Owen's face is tucked into Avril's neck and he can feel her pulse, smell the warm scent of her perfume.

'I'm not sure Sebastian would altogether approve of this. It's not quite what he had in mind for us.'

'I know. Still, he's not here, thank goodness.'

'Too busy boiling some poor sod in oil, probably.'

'Does it frighten you?'

'What?'

'Dying.'

'Sometimes. I try not to think about it.'

'Yes, that's probably best,' she says, pulling away. She smiles. 'Thanks for the hug.'

Owen colours again. 'You're welcome. It's good to hug.'

'Ah, you're one of those.'

'What?'

'A new man, in touch with your feminine side.'

'There's nothing feminine about me,' he says defensively.

She strokes his arm. 'Relax. It was a compliment, not a criticism. You're a good hugger. Right. I'll just go and slip into something more waterproof. Meet you back here in five minutes?'

Owen holds the door open for her and the girl steps through. 'Okay, great. We could walk along the cliff and check out that albatross.'

'Trust me, Owen, it's a gull,' she says, and her scornful laughter echoes down the hallway as she makes her way back to her room.

Smiling to himself, Owen scoops up his sweater from the back of a small, cane chair and pulls it over his head, blindfolding him. He is struggling to insert his arms into the sleeves when he hears someone enter the room. There's a tap on his shoulder and he turns to face them. 'That was quick. Did you forget something?' He can just make out a shadowy figure through the tightly woven yarn of the garment and assumes it's Avril. Hands reach out towards him. They take hold of the sweater's close-fitting neckline and pull it down off his head. Owen is horrified to find himself face to face with Sebastian, their noses almost touching; his hands at Owen's throat.

'Oh Jesus!' cries Owen, and tries to duck out of the encircling hands, but he slips and falls to his knees with a groan. His face is now uncomfortably close to Sebastian's crotch.

'O-wen, I hoped you'd be pleased to see me, but I wasn't expecting this warm a welcome.'

'Oh Christ!' Owen does a quick about-turn and scuttles off towards the window on all fours, to the accompaniment of Sebastian's raucous laughter.

'Oh, you prefer it doggy-style, do you?' he calls after him.

Owen scrambles to his feet and stands with his back to the window. 'What are you doing here?' he says nervously.

'Well, I came back to see if Avril had had any luck in stiffening your resolve, but I don't think that was a handkerchief you had in your pocket just now.'

'I've got nothing in my trousers believe me.'

'Oh, I think you have Owen. Perhaps you'd like me to check it's still there, put your mind at rest.'

'Look, just stop mucking about, will you. I've told you, I'm not like that.'

'So you say.' Sebastian's eyes narrow. 'Still, something stirs methinks. You thought I was someone else just now, didn't you? The fair Agnes perhaps. Could it be? Have we scored a hole in one. Put the ball in the back of the net. Potted the black. Come on, Owen, don't be shy. You can tell your Uncle Sebbie.'

Owen tries to avoid Sebastian's penetrating gaze but those eyes of his are mesmerising and he can't look away. 'Uh, not exactly,' he mumbles.

The dark eyes glitter and Owen knows that this is when Sebastian is at his most dangerous. 'And what *exactly* does that mean – everything but actual penetration?'

'Not quite.'

This draws an impatient sigh from his interrogator. 'Not quite. So, what are we talking about here… heavy petting unclothed?' Owen shakes his head. 'Partially clothed then?' Another shake of the head. 'Fully clothed? Fire and brimstone, Owen! It's been three weeks. Have you made any progress at all while I've been away?'

Owen hesitates. Should he invent something, spin Sebastian a yarn in order to placate him? As long as he keeps it simple, it might work. He could pretend that the hug he has just enjoyed with Avril took place between him and Agnes; that the peck on the cheek was a full blown kiss on the lips…

'Well,' he begins, but one glance at his interrogator's stern countenance and Owen's resolve fails him. Sebastian can see right through him and he has always been an unconvincing liar. He is damned whatever he says, so he might as well tell the truth and get it over with. Besides these 'cat and mouse' games of Sebastian's are more than his shaky nerves can stand.

'None to speak of, no,' he admits quietly, and waits nervously for Sebastian's considerable wrath to descend upon him. But not for the first time in their brief acquaintance, Sebastian surprises him by doing the unexpected. Instead of exploding, the dark angel thoughtfully strokes his chiselled chin.

'It wasn't Agnes you mistook me for just now, was it?' Owen looks stricken but says nothing. Spinning on his heel Sebastian marches to the door and throws it wide.

'Avril, get in here, now!' he barks, his voice reverberating down the hallway. He comes back in to the room to find Owen pulling on his waterproof. 'And where do you think you're going?' He snaps at him.

'A walk . . ?' Owen suggests, more in hope than with any conviction.

'Take it off!' orders Sebastian, 'You're not going anywhere. I haven't finished with you yet.'

Trembling now, Owen quickly shrugs the jacket off his shoulders. He shrinks back as Sebastian approaches him and throws an arm around his shoulder; frog-marches him towards the window. Owen fears he may be about to throw him through it, but at the window he swings him round and walks him down to the middle of the bedroom.

'Owen, have you any idea what the Boss will do to you, or me for that matter, if you fail him, umm? Just think Hieronymus Bosch and multiply it by ten. Vlad the Impaler is a pussy cat by comparison.'

'Is? You mean he's down there too?'

Sebastian nods. 'He's one of the Boss's chief lieutenants and still up to his old tricks.' He smiles grimly. 'Difference is, you're stuck like a pig for ever... eternal agony. Not nice, Owen. Not nice at all.'

Owen shudders. 'Not nice? It's appalling.'

'*Impaling* Owen, it's called impaling. So, if you don't want to spend eternity as a Kebab, I suggest you work at improving your seduction technique. Now would be a good time to start.'

'But how?' says Owen miserably. 'I can't just grab the poor woman and throw her down on the bed.'

Sebastian tightens his grip on Owen's shoulders and squeezes him with a force that threatens to crack his ribs.

'Why not?' he rumbles. 'Sounds pretty good to me. Lacking in subtlety perhaps, but it would certainly make your intentions towards the lady clear. Set the hare running, as it were. There's a lot to be said for a strong man who knows what he wants.'

'She's just not up for it,' he says vehemently. 'She's not that kind of girl.'

Sebastian releases Owen from his grip and brushes the creases out of his new sweater. 'Tell me something Owen. Would you prefer to be marinated in hot chilli sauce or a nice drop of virgin's blood?'

There's a tap on the door and Avril, wearing a red anorak, stands in the doorway. 'You wanted to see me?' she says. Outwardly the girl appears cool and collected but a slight twitch at the corner of her right eye betrays her nervousness.

'Ah, Avril my dear, do come in,' Sebastian says in welcome; the words flowing over his tongue like warm oil. 'Owen and I have just been having a little catch up. Not much has been happening on the Agnes front, apparently. What's your assessment of the situation?' Avril and Owen exchange anxious glances. 'No, don't look at him. Well?'

'I'd say that about sums it up. Yes. Broadly speaking.'

'Well now, it seems we're all agreed on that point at least. Thank you, Avril. That will be all for the moment.' His language remains reasonable and considered but there's a hint of menace now in the tone.

'It's not entirely Owen's fault, you know. Agnes would be a challenge for any…'

But Sebastian interrupts her. 'You're still here Avril, why is that?' he states icily.

'Because…' she pauses as if reconsidering her

decision to speak up then, taking a deep breath, plunges on, 'because I must take some of the responsibility for what has happened or rather, hasn't happened while I've been here,' she says.

Owen mouths the word *go*, or is it *no*, Avril can't be sure; the shape formed by his lips is the same. Sebastian eyeballs Avril as if trying to read her mind then brings his cold gaze to bear on his protégé. 'So that's the way it is, all girls together. Interesting...' he says, his eyes still fixed on Owen. 'Very well, you can stay, but be aware, that sharing responsibility for this fiasco with our reluctant Casanova here has consequences for *all* those involved. Sit down both of you,' he orders and, leaving them to perch themselves on the bed, brings the bedroom's one chair over and straddles it back to front. Resting his chin on his folded arms Sebastian glowers at them. 'Well my dears, before we go any further is there anything you'd like to tell me?' He looks expectantly from one to the other.

The pair stare blankly back at him, the ensuing silence broken only by the distant cries of the gulls as they wheel and dive above the cliff top.

'There's nothing *to* tell. That's the problem, isn't it?' says Avril finally, as Sebastian shows no sign of continuing.

Sebastian's chin comes up, and he straightens himself like a cobra rising from its basket. 'Now you see, that's just the sort of thing I'm talking about. I ask you a question and you answer it with one of your own. Some might think that you're being somewhat defensive.'

'And some might say I'm just pointing out the bleeding obvious,' she retorts boldly.

At her side Owen winces. He admires the girl's spirit,

wishes he had her courage, but can't help feeling that her outbursts can only make things far worse for both of them. They were in enough trouble as it was and, faced with an angry snake, you don't go poking him with a sharpened stick. But this snake has cunning; he doesn't lash out blindly, he is prepared to wait for just the right moment before he strikes.

'What about you Owen, anything you want to add?'

Owen would love to match Avril's ballsy display of bravado but ever the realist, he shakes his head. He knows it's cowardly of him, that he should be protecting the girl, not the other way round, but wonders if she would be as brave if Sebastian had thrown her off the Hyatt's roof.

'Well then, I suggest that the two of you go for a long walk and think about your future, because as things stand neither of you appear to have one.'

6: THE LONELY SEA AND THE SKY

They have been walking along the beach, the shingle crunching beneath their feet, for twenty minutes without a word passing between them. The silence is becoming unbearable and Owen is the first to break it. 'Thanks for sticking up for me, but you shouldn't have.'

The ghost of a smile plays briefly upon Avril's lips. 'That's okay; I'm a long-time supporter of lost causes. I would pick the loser even if it was a one horse race.' Owen laughs. 'What?' she says. 'Oh, I'm sorry Owen, I didn't mean…'

'Yes you did. Forget it. I am a loser. Do you think it's something we become or are we born that way?'

She slips her arm between his and gives it a squeeze. 'There wouldn't be any winners without losers, you know.'

'My brother must be so grateful for me.' Owen says, and laughing, they continue their walk arm-in-arm as if they were carefree lovers, and not the doomed participants in a game of Russian roulette in which all the chambers are loaded.

Ahead of them a small break has appeared in an otherwise uniformly grey sky; a glimmer of light amongst all the gloom. Scrambling up the slippery shingle still wet from the rain, they step onto the coastal path and walk towards the light. The going is easier here, but their pace remains leisurely as neither of them is in any hurry to get back to the sea-front house or Sebastian Tantalus. To their right, regimented rows of static caravans have been planted in what was once a farmer's field. Some of the proud owners have added a sun-deck so that they can soak up the sun, without having to mix with the lesser mortals at the beach, just a few yards beyond the wire fence which separates them. Two hardy caravaners, grimly determined to man the sun-deck despite the inclement weather, wave to them as they pass.

'How very Bwitish,' says Owen under his breath, as he and Avril wave back, 'We've got a sun-deck and we're going to jolly well sit out on it, even on a rotten day like this.'

Avril detects a note of bitterness in his voice and suspects that Owen is not referring solely to the weather; though she does wonder if even now, her companion fully appreciates the danger they are in. Sebastian might be a lot of things but he was no kidder and he would insist upon having his pound of flesh.

'We need to talk,' she tells him.

Owen looks mildly surprised. 'Do we? But we're alright, aren't we? I did say I was sorry.'

'Yes, yes. We're fine. I was referring to the Agnes situation.'

'Oh, that.'

'Yes *that*. You have to take what Sebastian said seriously. He may have been smiling when he said it, but believe me he wasn't happy. You're in big trouble and so am I, thanks to my big mouth.'

They are approaching a wooden bench and Avril suggests that they sit down for a moment. A small brass plaque informs them that the bench was donated in memory of the late Arthur Herbert by his widow Frances. The small patch of light has grown much larger while they've been walking and, aided by a light breeze, it is slowly spreading westwards, promising a lighter evening. The number of people down on the beach has also increased and there are children playing in the rock pools.

'Look, I'm sorry you've been dragged into this mess, but there's no way that woman is jumping into bed with me or any other man for that matter.'

'You think Agnes prefers women?'

'NO! Maybe, I don't know. She's very religious, that one. If I had long hair, a beard and my name was Jesus she'd want to marry me – the woman's practically a nun for crying out loud!'

Owen, his face a picture of misery, is staring blankly out to sea as if the answer to his problem is out there and about to pop up over the horizon. Avril takes hold of his face and turns it towards hers.

'Nevertheless,' she tells him, looking him straight in the eye, 'the lady has to put out for you. It's just sex, Owen, she's not going to die, but you are if you don't deliver!' She gives him a wink. 'You never know, she might enjoy it.'

'Oh yeah, and how do I perform that little miracle?'

Avril rolls her eyes. 'You send her flowers. You take

her out for a meal. You make sure she takes lots of vodka with her holy water – whatever it takes – you do it.' Her companion laughs. 'I'm serious Owen… or, do you want to spend the rest of eternity as the main ingredient in Sebastian's recipe for Coq au vin?'

'God no! I hate foreign food.'

It's Avril's turn to laugh. 'Bang goes the French restaurant then.' She gives his hand an affectionate squeeze. 'Owen, you're priceless!'

'You know, it's funny. When Sebastian dragged me down to that awful club you work in, I wanted nothing to do with you. But now I've got to know you better, I wish it was you I had to seduce.'

'Why? Because I'm easy?' she says without rancour.

'No. God no, I didn't mean…' A sudden impulse seizes him and taking her face in both hands, he brings his mouth down hard on hers. Her lips are as soft and as yielding as they look, but he has little time to appreciate them before Avril pushes him away.

'Christ, Owen, what the hell are you doing?' she screeches at him as she jumps up off the bench.

Owen doesn't know quite what to say; he doesn't understand what just happened either. He feels foolish now, but a second ago it had seemed a perfectly natural thing for him to do. He'd experienced this sudden rush of feeling for the girl and had acted on it. 'Avril I'm so sorry,' He seemed to have done nothing but apologise to her since she got here. 'I just…'

'You just what… thought you'd grab a quickie while you still could?'

'No! I… it was just a kiss,' he says miserably.

'Well, take a tip from an expert on these matters,

don't go lunging at Agnes like that or she'll run a mile.' Owen looks utterly crestfallen; like a little boy who's been sent to sit on the naughty step. That wife of his must have ripped the guts out of him, thinks Avril. She can't help feeling sorry for him; he is completely out of his depth – why couldn't Sebastian see that and set him an easier task? 'Come on, lover boy,' she says in a conciliatory tone, 'we'd better get back to the house. I can outline our master plan to Sebastian while you're phoning Agnes.'

Owen consults his watch. 'She won't be back from church yet.'

'When she gets back from church then,' she tells him firmly, 'you phone her and say you'd like to take her out for a meal, somewhere nice.' She takes hold of his arm and pulls him to his feet. 'Come on, Owen, you can do this,' she says with a good deal more conviction than she feels.

*

Owen ends his call to Agnes with a whispered 'Bye.' There's a tap on his bedroom door and Avril slips into the room. He drops the mobile onto the bed beside him.

'How did it go?' she asks.

'Fine, I suppose. I'm seeing her tomorrow evening,' he informs her, his voice a drab monotone.

'You don't sound too happy about it.'

Owen lies back on the bed, clasps his hands behind his head. 'Well, nothing's changed, has it, since I last saw her. I'm still me, she's still Saint Agnes…'

'That's the spirit, Owen. Onwards and upwards,' says Avril scathingly. 'You'll like my news even less, Sebastian wants to see you.'

'Oh shit, what about?'

'Boy's talk,' she says in a stage whisper.

'Great. That's all I need, another lecture from our resident expert on the birds and the bees!'

'Well, you've only got yourself to blame for that. Grow a pair, will you. You're not the only one who's being inconvenienced here.' And leaving Owen with that jibe ringing in his ears, Avril flounces off to phone her mother, who won't be pleased to learn that Sebastian wants her daughter to stay on for a while longer.

At the lounge door Owen hesitates for a moment then, lightly rapping on the door with the back of his hand, he enters. Sebastian is stood in front of the fireplace with his back to him. He turns and smiles benignly. In his left hand he holds an open book. It's a small, slim hardback with a faded green cover.

'The Tragical History of Dr. Faustus,' he says without any prompting from Owen. 'Ever read it?'

'No, can't say I have.' Owen has never heard of this Dr. Faustus, but doesn't wish to show his ignorance.

'Oh, you should. You really should. You will find it most illuminating.' He closes the book with a snap. 'Here, take it and make sure you read it.'

Reluctantly Owen closes the gap between them and takes the book from him. Turning it over in his hands, he flicks through the first few pages. 'It's a play?'

'Well spotted, Owen,' Sebastian says dryly. 'There are no descriptive flights of fancy; gets straight on with it, d'ya see? Which is what you should have done with the fair Agnes.'

Owen ignores the dig. 'Christopher Marlowe... is he

one of your recruits?' he asks.

Sebastian shakes his head. 'Sadly no, he didn't need any help from us. His friend Shakespeare on the other hand…'

Now, Owen has heard of William Shakespeare, they'd done him at school; he just hadn't been aware that he was a mate of this guy Marlowe. 'Shakespeare, really? Wow!

'Yes, wow… precisely.' Sebastian says sniffily. 'One of the greatest, if not *the* greatest writers in the English language and, four hundred years after his death, his plays are still being performed all over the world.'

'So, what did he have to do to… you know, qualify?

'Well, not to give too much away,' he says in the hushed tones of a conspirator, 'Our friend Kit Marlowe didn't live long enough to write more than a handful of plays and poems. You get my drift?' he taps the side of his nose.

'Wow!'

'Wow, again? As an expression of one's amazement I find it somewhat limited,' Sebastian points out with evident disdain for his companion's inadequate vocabulary. 'I do hope you're going to be a little more imaginative when it comes to sweet-talking Agnes into bed.' Delving into the inside pocket of his jacket, he brings out a silver, art deco cigarette case; opens it and, without offering one to Owen, takes out a cigarette. Closing the case, he tamps down any loose strands of tobacco; tapping both ends of the cigarette on the lid. Placing the cigarette between his lips, he lights up with nothing more than a snap of his fingers.

'A curious habit this, but one I've grown rather fond

of,' he says, blowing several smoke rings into the air. Owen wonders if he should point out that there is a sign in the hallway which expressly forbids guests to smoke in the house. He decides against it; why would Sebastian give a toss about house rules? Why would he give a toss about anything? What possible sanctions can be imposed on an immortal being? Owen might just as well warn Sebastian not to smoke because it was bad for his health.

As if to emphasise the point, his nemesis flicks his cigarette ash into the open fireplace, most of which is occupied by a large, log burning stove. He settles himself in a fireside armchair and signals Owen to sit down in an identical chair on the opposite side of the slate hearth. Hanging above the fireplace is a large Jack Vettriano print; a man in shirtsleeves, holding aloft a black umbrella to shade them both from the sun, is chatting up a young woman in a red, polka-dot dress. They are leaning against the decorative railings on an unidentified seaside promenade. For the first time, Owen takes note of the print's title; *Bad Boy, Good Girl*. If only he was the bad boy, he thinks; it would make seducing Agnes so much easier. Failing that what he could really do with right now is a stiff drink, but Sebastian shows no inclination to play the genial host; signalling that they are here solely to discuss the business at hand. The two contemplate each other across the hearth; Sebastian like a predator eying up its next meal, Owen returning his gimlet stare like the proverbial rabbit caught in the headlights.

Sebastian is the first to break the spell. 'Well, Owen, it seems we have reached a crossroads, you and me. Let's hope the plan of action you and the lovely Avril have come up with will take you in the right direction. If not…'

he leaves the implied threat hanging in the air and takes a long draw on his cigarette, pushing the smoke out through his nostrils. Fire and brimstone personified. 'I must be honest; I do have some reservations as to the likelihood of its success and, bearing in mind that failure is no longer an option...' Another pause for that message to sink in. 'Nevertheless, I am prepared to back your plan, subject to one proviso.'

Owen, whose own enthusiasm for the plan has all but evaporated whilst Sebastian has been talking, can barely bring himself to ask the obvious question, 'What's that, then?' he asks with some trepidation.

Sebastian takes a last drag on his cigarette and tosses the smoking butt behind the log burner. 'That I am there to put an end to your dithering. You're going to do the deed this time, if I have to lift you onto the lady myself!'

Owen gives a nervous laugh. 'Are you serious?' he says, almost choking, 'She's not going to do it with you there.' She is unlikely to do it with just me there either, he thinks, but doesn't give voice to his doubts.

'She won't see me, I'll be invisible,' Sebastian assures him. 'Look, it's that or it's Kebab a la Owen for the next trillion years.'

'It's no good, I can't do it with you there.'

'Can't or won't? Do you know how long we marinate someone like you, eh? A thousand years. Imagine it, a thousand years pickling in a hot chilli sauce. Ummm, won't you taste yummy? So, what's it to be; a spot of how's-your-father, or a nice long soak in something hot and spicy?'

Given the nature of the choices, there was only one decision Owen could make. 'Alright, alright, but in my own time, I'm not a rapist.'

'That's the last thing anyone would ever accuse you of being, my dear. You just need to be firm with her, that's all.' Sebastian grins lasciviously, 'Firm… yes, I like the sound of that.'

'You're a pervert, you know that, don't you?'

'Compliments, Owen? Whatever next?'

'Just don't get in the way. The situation's difficult enough as it is, without you looking over my shoulder.'

'Oh, you're shy. How sweet,' he coos. Sebastian reaches over the arm of his chair and retrieves a bottle of whisky from a small table at the side of his chair. 'Will you join me for a nightcap, Owen?'

A little earlier Owen would have killed for a shot of whisky, but now all he wants is to escape to his room; to get away from Sebastian and his smart alec remarks. So he declines the offer of a drink and, clutching the book and what's left of his dignity, bids Sebastian good night.

On the landing Owen pauses to listen outside Avril's bedroom door. They had parted on a sour note and he would like to make it up with her, but he can hear her talking to her son on her mobile. From the sound of it, it's going to be a long conversation and with a leaden heart he moves on down the hallway to his own room. His room is almost dark but, before switching on the light and closing the curtains, he crosses to the window and takes a last look at the sea. A glimmer of light is still visible in the west, a thin strip of silver separating the rolling dark sea and the advancing night. Owen watches until sea and sky become one, then pulling the curtains to, he turns away from the window and switches on the anglepoise lamp at his bedside.

Having nothing better to do than dwell on his miseries, Owen takes the book to bed and, propped up on one elbow, begins reading *The Tragical History of Dr Faustus*. Only two pages in and he is already wondering why Sebastian was so keen that he should read the thing; it's boring and large chunks of the text are in Latin, but he perseveres and a couple of pages further in a line jumps out at him: *"The reward of sin is death: that's hard."*

But he really sits up and takes notice when Mephistopheles appears and proclaims he is a servant to great Lucifer. It's then that the penny drops and all becomes clear; substitute Owen Leadbeater for Faustus and Sebastian Tantalus for Mephistopheles and their stories are the same. From that moment Owen is gripped by Marlowe's narrative, and is still reading as the house grows quiet around him and his companions settle down to sleep.

It's two o'clock in the morning when Faustus, begging for mercy, is dragged off to hell by Mephistopheles and other un-named devils. By which time Owen has so identified himself with the character that he feels traumatised. Faustus' fate is ultimately Owen's fate too, and the realisation is a sobering one. With a shudder he closes the book, as if in doing so he can shut out the terrors that fill his mind. But they remain and, like a cancer, grow inside him, fed by his overactive imagination.

Owen switches off the bedside lamp and slides down under the bedcovers, but within minutes he switches the lamp back on again. Thanks to Sebastian and his damned book, the darkness now holds too many terrors for him; he daren't so much as close his eyes. Moonlight filtering through the curtains throws spectral shadows across the ceiling and the sound of the ebbing tide sucking at the sand becomes the slavering of demon jaws, eager to suck him down to eternal torment. Though he draws some comfort from the lamp's friendly glow, it doesn't entirely erase these disturbing visions nor banish the abject terror that has suddenly overtaken him. All he can do now, Owen decides, is lie there with the light on until the sun comes up and hope that the new day will dispel these fears as easily as it does the night.

But he does fall asleep eventually, in spite of everything. It's a troubled slumber, however, filled with Hammer Horror images of the charnel house and accompanied by the pungent smell of roasting flesh and hot chilli sauce. He wakes up in a cold sweat to find the bedside lamp still alight and sunlight blazing through the curtains. Owen snatches up his wristwatch from the bedside table; it's still only seven o'clock. On any other day he would fall back against the pillows and stay there till nine, but he doesn't feel like doing that today. He is still troubled by his night time fears and that makes him restless.

Clicking off the bedside lamp and throwing back the covers, Owen sits up and swings his skinny, white legs over the edge of the bed. Slumped forward, he cradles his weary head in his hands; pausing for a moment to collect his thoughts, before launching himself into what could be the most significant day of his life. Pulling on the crumpled clothes he wore yesterday and carrying his shoes, he silently creeps downstairs. In the hallway he slips his stockinged feet into the brown leather casuals and ties the laces. Then, ears straining for the slightest sounds of movement from above, he carefully slides back the bolt and opening the front door, steps out into the bright morning sunshine. Walking briskly, he crosses the seafront road, pausing on the other side to check for any sign of movement at the windows of his temporary home, before taking the concrete steps down to the beach.

The shingle is wet and slippery with seaweed stranded by the retreating tide. He carefully picks his way over it and onto the narrow strip of sandy beach that separates sea from shingle. Head down, hands stuffed in his pockets, he strides off with the intention of putting as much distance as he can between himself and the seafront house. Up on the promenade, the sunlight had been warm, but down here on the shoreline a cool breeze means it's much colder and he regrets not wearing his Kagool.

For a while Owen has the beach all to himself but gradually, as the sun rises higher in the sky, he is joined by early morning dog-walkers and joggers. Above his head, the sea birds wheel and dive; squabble over tidbits of food left behind by yesterday's picnickers; their cries sounding shrill and sharp above the soft lapping of the surf and the bass barking of the excited canines. He stops to pick up an interesting looking shell and, turning it over in his hands, is reminded of the evening when Sebastian introduced him to the dubious delights of eating oysters. That was the night this nightmare he calls his life had begun. It seems like years ago now; he can barely remember the time when he led what most people would regard as being a normal life. And now it all came down to this one last chance to avoid an early death and eternal damnation. It will only postpone the inevitable for another thirty years or so, of course, but at this precise moment, for Owen that seems to be an awfully long time away. After all, in the final analysis, it was every man for himself, wasn't it? Agnes would just have to take her chances the same as everybody else on the planet. You can't afford to be noble, he tells himself, you're just as entitled to three score years and ten as anybody else.

The decision made to sacrifice the virgin and not himself, he takes the shell and hurls it spinning into the sea.

7: AND THE DEVIL MAKES THREE

The evening had begun well enough. Dead-on-the-dot of seven, Owen, clutching a bouquet of tulips, was at Agnes's front door; a flat above her shop in the high street. He had intended to present her with a dozen red roses but had switched on Avril's advice. "Most girls I know think that red roses are naff," she had told him. Roses or tulips, he still felt self-conscious carrying them through the streets as he walked up into the town. Agnes had seemed pleased with them, at any rate – Avril had been right about that at least. For this first part of the evening he is going solo; "You're on your own until you get back to her flat," Sebastian assured him, but Owen still had the feeling of being followed all the way into town.

Now, sat opposite Agnes in the restaurant, Owen is only slightly more relaxed. Agnes is looking so different from her usual self. On all Owen's frequent visits to her shop, she has worn her mousey-coloured hair in a tight bun and sported a pair of outsized tortoise-shell spectacles. Tonight, she has her hair down around her shoulders and the glasses are gone; replaced, he presumes, by contact lenses. The shapeless Kaftans and summer smocks have been dropped for a smart, three-quarter length, black dress. And most surprising of all, Agnes is wearing make-up; a warm tan blusher and red lipstick! Most men would find this encouraging, but in this guise she reminds Owen so much of his ex-wife Maureen – she even has the same cornflower blue eyes – it's disconcerting.

Becoming aware that Owen is staring at her intently, Agnes, who is about to pop another prawn into her mouth, lowers her fork. 'What is it?' she asks, snatching up her napkin, 'Have I got some sauce on my face?' Owen assures her that she hasn't. 'What is it, then?' she wonders.

'Nothing, I've just realised you're wearing make-up, that's all.'

The blusher on Agnes's cheeks deepens a shade. 'I wondered how long it would be before you noticed,' she says with little girl coyness.

'I knew there was something different about you, but I couldn't quite put my finger on what it was until just now,' Owen confesses, and feels his own cheeks burn with embarrassment. This admission brings with it the inescapable fact that he has been so wrapped up in his own thoughts; that he has paid very little attention to his dinner date. Once again he is forcibly reminded that his life depends on the evening coming to a successful conclusion. What was it Avril had told him? *"The best way to get a girl into bed is to make her laugh."* Well, so far he'd come closer to making Agnes cry than laugh. In danger of drifting off into his own thoughts once more, he tries desperately to think of something witty and amusing to say. Playing for time, he spears another segment of melon and conveys it to his mouth. Though he tries to make it last as long as possible, the small piece of melon seems to melt on his tongue and is gone before he can come up with a suitably funny remark. He is spared any further racking of his brains by an intervention from Agnes.

'Are you alright? What's the matter, don't you like my make-up?' The cornflower blue eyes look troubled.

'No. I mean yes. You look very nice.' As a compliment it's polite at best, but he'd been caught off guard and, in his scramble to retrieve the situation, it was the best he could come up with. 'How's your prawn cocktail?' he asks in a clumsy attempt to change the subject. The cuisine is only one step above pub grub, but the restaurant is small and intimate with subdued lighting and a red glass bowl on each table has a Tea Light candle floating inside it, the tablecloths are clean and the menu is in English.

'It's fine,' she replies frostily, bringing the conversation to an abrupt end.

The pair eat the remainder of their starters in silence. Alarmed at how quickly his carefully laid plan has come to grief, Owen wonders what he can possibly do now to salvage the evening. An opportunity presents itself when Agnes excuses herself from the table to powder her nose, as she delicately puts it, though Owen suspects she may well be going to check her make-up as well. He suddenly recalls Sebastian's cynical advice of the night before and summoning the waitress – a short, chubby faced girl with a purple streak in her hair – orders a double vodka. When it arrives he checks no one is looking his way, then tips the double shot into his companion's glass of apple and mango juice. He feels bad about spiking Agnes's drink but the stakes are high and desperate measures are called for if he is to avoid calamity.

'We seem to have got off on the wrong foot,' Owen tells her, when Agnes returns to their table. 'And in case I didn't make myself clear earlier, I think you look terrific in make-up,' he adds for good measure. His companion smiles. 'So, do you think we could rewind and start again?' he asks.

Agnes laughs, a sound like the tinkling of wind chimes. 'Of course,' she says.

Owen raises his beer glass. Agnes does the same with her vodka-laced apple and mango juice. 'To a fresh start,' Owen proposes and they bring their glasses together with a clink.

After a few more swigs from her supercharged fruit juice Agnes becomes positively jolly and, on his second pint, Owen too is beginning to enjoy himself; the fears and uncertainties hanging over his future all but forgotten. The rest of the meal goes so well – Agnes unknowingly imbibing a second vodka and orange – that the pair leave the restaurant arm-in-arm. They chat all the way back to Agnes's front door and she is still giggling over something Owen has just said as she turns the key and steps into the tiny hallway. Inviting him in for a coffee, she starts up the long flight of stairs.

Owen is about to follow her but freezes, when an all too familiar voice whispers in his ear, 'It's Showtime!' Sebastian announces dramatically.

'Christ Sebastian!' rasps a startled Owen. 'Do you have to creep up on people like that?'

'What's that?' Agnes calls from the landing.

'Nothing, just bumped into a friend on the doorstep.'

'Does he want to come in for coffee too?' Agnes enquires. Sebastian grins wolfishly.

'No, it's alright. He's got to get home,' Owen calls up to her, then in a hoarse whisper to Sebastian. 'I'm begging you, please, just leave me to it. I can handle this on my own.'

'Oh, no, no, no this is far too important a ssh-matter to leave you to your own vices – I mean, de-vices.' Sebastian tells him, vigorously wagging an admonishing finger in front of Owen's face.

Owen stares at his nemesis in disbelief; the dark angel is slurring his words and seems a little unsteady on his feet; it's as if he is swaying to the strains of some inaudible refrain. 'Have you been drinking?' Owen asks.

Sebastian gives him a sheepish grin. 'I may have had a drinky-poo or two while staking you two out at the restaurant.' He has great difficulty in pronouncing this last word; his tongue twisting around it and tying itself in several knots before he says it correctly.

'You were there? Where? I didn't see you.'

'I was the fat little man shat at the table in the corner by the bar,' Sebastian informs him with undisguised pride.

'But we agreed that I would be flying solo for the first part of the evening,' says Owen angrily. In his righteous indignation at Sebastian's breach of their agreement, Owen has overlooked the full significance of what his companion has just said, but then the light bulb lights up and alarm bells begin ringing. 'You can change your appearance at will?'

'Of course. This… ,' he runs both hands down his

torso, 'is just a convenient shell; an acceptable disguise. We don't want to go round frightening the children, now, do we?'

The revelation that Sebastian can, like a chameleon, assume any guise he chooses has worrying implications. From now on, how can Owen be sure that when he confides in Avril, for instance, that he isn't in fact opening up his heart to one of Sebastian's many Avatars? Owen's mood rapidly swings back to its default setting – pessimistic. He has never been too well acquainted with Lady Luck but this evening she has been exceedingly fickle. It was ironic really that, having managed to avert disaster without any help from Sebastian, it is his mentor who is now the problem. What chance has he got of seducing Agnes with an invisible drunk bumping into the furniture, just as he is about to make his killer move?

Agnes reappears at the top of the stairs. 'Owen, are you coming up or not?' She peers down into the stairwell. 'What are you doing down there? What happened to your friend?'

Owen turns to Sebastian still standing beside him. It is true, then – he is invisible to anybody but himself. 'He had to go,' he says with some vehemence. But refusing to take the hint, Sebastian just winks at Owen; a comic exaggeration and gives him an inane grin.

'Suit yourself,' Owen mutters under his breath and, closing the street door, trots up the stairs to join Agnes who is waiting for him on the landing. 'Sorry about that,' says Owen. 'One of the friends I'm staying with. Couldn't get rid of him,' he adds for Sebastian's benefit. 'Always poking his nose in where it's not wanted.' He glances back down the way he has come but can't see him anywhere;

wonders if Sebastian has made himself invisible even to him or has thought better of joining them and gone home.

At first glance Agnes's lounge appears to be more like a stock room for the shop downstairs. Three of the room's walls are lined with piles of books; most of them religious in nature, judging by the titles. Only the area around the fireplace has been kept clear; a cosy two-seater sofa and an easy chair marking the boundary.

'Make yourself at home,' says Agnes and pats the back of the sofa. 'I'll just get the coffee.'

Owen waits until his date is in the kitchen then, hurrying back to the hallway, begins searching for Sebastian in the other rooms that comprise Agnes's one bedroom flat. He checks the bathroom first, then swiftly moves on to her bedroom; a Spartan affair that wouldn't look out of place in a nunnery. There's a single bed, a cheap bedside table with an anglepoise lamp, a framed print of Holman Hunt's *The Light of the World* and a dreary looking wardrobe circa 1950. He is about to search the latter – it being the only place in the room where Sebastian might hope to hide – when he hears Agnes calling. He can't be caught searching her bedroom; that would have her thinking he is some kind of pervert and bring this romantic evening to an abrupt and ignominious end. Racing back to the bathroom, he hurriedly flushes the lavatory and swills his hands under the running tap. He doesn't have time to dry them properly on the hand towel hanging on a ring beside the basin, and is still wiping them on his handkerchief as he returns to the lounge.

'Oh, there you are,' says Agnes, without turning round. 'I was beginning to think you'd gone home like your friend.'

Owen quickly stuffs his soggy handkerchief into his trouser pocket. 'Sorry, desperate for the loo – shouldn't have had that second pint,' he explains.

'Well, you're here now. Sit down and drink your coffee before it gets cold.'

Owen joins Agnes on the sofa and she hands him a mug of black coffee. Owen helps himself to milk and sugar from a tea-tray set out on the pine coffee table that completes the lounge furnishings. Like the rest of the furniture in the flat none of it matches but consists of odds and sods bought second hand or handed down from relatives or friends. The sofa is yellow fabric with a brown floral pattern, the chair wing-backed and red velour.

'Nice flat,' Owen comments for want of something better to say. Secretly he thinks it's rather sad. There's nothing cosy or homely about it; rather like his own place, he reflects gloomily. Admittedly, it's nobody's fault but his own; he should have done more to put his stamp on the place after his mother died, but the blackness that descended upon him after her death, coming on top of the divorce from Maureen and then being made redundant, had left him too full of self-pity and self-loathing to do much about it.

Owen is trying to think of something more constructive to say when the silence is broken by a loud bump. It seems to come from the bedroom.

'What was that?' Agnes asks, visibly alarmed.

'What was what?' replies a poker-faced Owen. 'I didn't hear anything.' He assumes that what they've just heard was the sound of Sebastian falling out of the wardrobe, or bumping into Agnes's bed or some other solid object. Whatever it was he can't acknowledge

Sebastian's presence in the flat to Agnes.

'You must have done.' She stares at Owen, a look of utter disbelief on her face. 'You really didn't hear a thing?'

Owen doesn't bat an eyelid. 'No, nothing,' he lies. 'But just to be sure, I'll go and take a look.' He is already on his feet and making for the door as he says this; anxious to get to Sebastian before Agnes decides to go and investigate the intrusion for herself.

Entering the bedroom, he closes the door behind him and turns on the light. 'Sebastian,' he whispers. 'Sebastian are you in here?' Receiving no answer, he crosses to the wardrobe and throwing the door open, peers inside. There's half a dozen or so of the floral summer dresses and smocks that Agnes favours, a smart two piece suit and a navy blue, winter coat. A vague smell of some musky perfume clings to these garments, but of Sebastian there is no sign. Owen waves his hand backwards and forwards between the hanging clothes just to make sure, but there's nothing between them but air. He may have convinced Agnes that she is hearing things, but Owen knows better; there's little room left for doubt after that bump in the night – Sebastian *is* in the flat – only now he is as invisible to Owen as he is to Agnes.

With many a nervous glance behind him, Owen returns to the lounge to report that he has found no signs of an intruder and, though strictly speaking this is true, he knows that one more sound from Sebastian will make a liar of him. Still, Agnes is visibly relieved to hear that she isn't being burgled and grateful for Owen's intervention. She pats the seat beside her, inviting Owen to re-join her on the sofa. She tops up his coffee, which in his absence has gone cold.

'What would you have done if there had been an intruder?' she asks.

'Oh… I don't know, I hadn't thought that far ahead.' What would he have done, he wonders, if instead of Sebastian he had been confronted by one of the local bad boys? Ordered him off the premises? Shut him in the bedroom and shouted to Agnes to call the police? But there had been no real likelihood of that happening and so, as far as Owen is concerned, the question is purely academic.

For Agnes, however, the question is a moral and ethical dilemma, the answers to which are to be found in the scriptures. She is enthusiastically quoting chapter and verse but Owen has tuned her out and is straining his ears to catch any extraneous sounds; the creak of a floorboard or the sound of Sebastian's breathing as he creeps about the room. It's all very reminiscent of Wells' novel *The Invisible Man* which Owen read and enjoyed several times as a boy, but though he is zoned in, he can hear nothing out of the ordinary. If only Agnes had a dog; canine hearing was far more acute than a human's and would detect Sebastian's presence long before he could.

'I'm so sorry Owen, I seem to be hogging the conversation. Please, jump in. I'd love to hear your view of Paul's pronouncement on thieves?'

Like a radio caught between stations, it takes Owen a moment to re-tune. 'Eh? Yes, well… I'm not sure there's a lot I can add to what you've already said.' Her long discourse has largely passed him by, and he has no idea what she is talking about. And who the hell was this Paul? Sebastian had made no mention of him.

'But you must have an opinion.' Agnes presses him.

'What Paul says in 1:Corinthians goes against Christ's teaching on forgiveness and redemption.'

Owen now realises that Corinthians is one of the many books to be found in the Bible, his knowledge of which is based on a handful of Sunday school attendances, and 1:Corinthians doesn't ring any bells. 'Yes, I suppose that is a bit awkward,' he says lamely.

'But can it really be right,' says Agnes with some fervour. 'That, "thieves will not enter the kingdom of heaven?"'

'Place is full of thieves.' The voice is Sebastian's not Owen's. The words were whispered but there is obviously not much wrong with Agnes's hearing.

Agnes stares open-mouthed at her companion. 'Owen... was that... you? I... I didn't see your lips move.'

Sebastian's sudden intervention renders Owen speechless. He glances over his left shoulder and there is his nemesis kneeling down behind him, his arms folded on the back of the sofa. The inane grin has gone, replaced by a scowl and he gives every appearance of being sober. Owen assumes that Agnes's diatribe has put that scowl on Sebastian's handsome visage, rather than exasperation at Owen's lack of progress with Agnes; though right now it's a moot point. More pressingly how does he explain the origin of that strange voice?

'Owen... what is it? What can you see over there?'

Agnes can only see him staring over his shoulder at the wall behind him. Relieved by her confirmation that Sebastian remains invisible to her, Owen turns to face her. He swallows hard, a garbled explanation of a long held desire to become a ventriloquist forming in his head. But, before he can get the words out, he receives a shove from

Sebastian which sends him sprawling into Agnes's lap, knocking the coffee cup out of her hand and spilling the contents over the front of her dress. Agnes lets out a startled cry and, pushing Owen away, leaps to her feet, frantically brushing at her sodden dress with both hands. Owen scrambles off the sofa and, pulling a white handkerchief from his trouser pocket, starts dabbing at her breasts with it.

'Leave this to me,' Agnes tells him, but Owen continues to dab and she brusquely brushes his hand away. 'Owen, just-leave-it,' she reiterates in a shriller tone.

Owen steps away, his face turning crimson, and stuffs the coffee stained handkerchief into his pocket. 'I'm so sorry. I don't know how that happened,' he says abjectly. 'I hope I haven't ruined your dress.' He feels obliged to apologise for Sebastian's wilful stupidity, but is baffled by it; what had he hoped to gain?

'Please don't fuss. It will be alright. It's washable. I just need to get out of this,' she says and, reaching behind her, unzips the dress. 'Sit down. I won't be a minute.'

Agnes hurries out of the room, Owen catching tantalising glimpses of naked flesh and black bra strap. As soon as the door closes, Owen confronts Sebastian.

'What the hell was that about?' he rasps. 'You made me look a right prat! And another thing; what's the point of making yourself invisible, if you're going to give a friggin' running commentary! This isn't reality TV.'

Sebastian, who is nonchalantly leaning against the wall, remains totally unruffled by Owen's tirade. 'Just moving things along, that's all. She's in the bedroom now peeling off that wet dress. If you're quick, you'll catch her in her bra and knickers.'

Owen rolls his eyes and shrugs his shoulders. 'Are you serious? You've just blown any chance I ever had of bedding her. Thanks to you, she thinks I'm a clumsy clown!'

Sebastian sheds his insouciance like a cloak as he straightens up off the wall. His dark eyes glitter like flint. 'Let's face it, Owen, you were never going to get her knickers off without some help from me. How you ever managed to get married is a mystery. No little Owens at home, is there?'

'Maureen couldn't have them; blocked fallopian tube, if you must know.'

'You're not firing blanks, then. Good. Perhaps your pistols jammed. Want Sebbie to take a look?'

'That won't be necessary. It's in perfect working order, thank you.'

Sebastian grabs Owen by the lapels. 'Is it?' he snarls. 'Well, try taking it out of its fucking holster then! Cos you're going to do this if I have to lift you onto the bloody woman myself.' Still holding Owen by the lapels, he swings him round and marches him towards the door. A few steps away from it, Sebastian moves his left hand up to Owen's throat and, squeezing it firmly, opens the door with his right. Spinning his captive around, he pushes him through the opening; giving him a hefty kick up the backside to send him on his way.

The pushing and shoving continues all the way down the hallway until they reach Agnes's bedroom door. 'Now, enough of this procrastination; get in there and get in *her*, or you're kebab meat.' With one last shove Sebastian propels Owen into the room.

Agnes, in bra, knickers and black tights, is standing

by the bed, dabbing at her damp chest with a blue hand towel. She looks up as Owen enters and her eyes widen with alarm. 'Owen! What are you doing in here?'

Owen halts in mid-stride. About to flee, he is once more seized from behind and thrown against the terrified Agnes, sending her toppling backwards onto the bed. Owen falls on top of her, his face between her breasts. Impelled by a mixture of fear and lust, he plants kisses on her breasts, her neck, her mouth.

But Agnes continues to protest, pleading with him to stop. Gradually the red mist that has temporarily fallen over Owen's eyes clears and he raises his head. One look at her panic-stricken face is enough to fill his eyes with tears of shame. What is happening to him? How could he, of all people, have come to this? No amount of wealth and fame could possibly justify the terror and humiliation he has just inflicted on her. Sick with self-loathing, Owen slowly gets up off the bed.

'I can't do this. I won't do this. It's not right,' he tells Sebastian.

Agnes doesn't move. She can't. Transfixed by fear, she wonders if she is going mad, as a second voice, higher pitched than Owen's and sounding slightly effeminate, gives a sharp response, 'You can't stop now,' it says from somewhere to the left of Owen.

'I can and I am,' says Owen boldly and, mouthing 'sorry' to Agnes, he turns as if to go. He takes just one step before his progress is blocked by some invisible barrier.

'Bad decision, Owen. Very bad decision,' intones the disembodied voice. 'This was your last chance and you've blown it my friend, *big time.*'

'You can do your worst. I don't care anymore. Now let me pass!'

'You stay right there. I'm not done with you yet. But first I have to make sure that Agnes here doesn't go running to the police.'

'Oh no, you're not going to…?' Owen just manages to stop himself saying 'kill her'. He doesn't want to freak Agnes out any more than she already is.

But Agnes has come to the same conclusion as Owen, and frantically digging her heels into the bedclothes, she tries to scrabble to the other side of the bed. She screams as unseen hands grip her ankles and drag her back.

'It's alright, Agnes, I'm not going to hurt you,' the voice assures her, and she finds herself looking up into the dark, unfathomable eyes of the most beautiful man she has ever seen. It's like staring at the face of an angel. 'Just lie still,' Sebastian says soothingly, 'It's been a long, hard day and you're feeling *very* sleepy.'

As the 'angel' continues to speak to her in the same soothing tones, Agnes feels her eyelids growing heavy and it becomes increasingly difficult to keep her eyes open. A few more minutes of this and she is fast asleep. Then, easing the duvet cover from under her limp body, Sebastian lifts Agnes up and, gently positioning her head on the pillow, pulls the covers over her. 'She'll remember nothing of this in the morning,' he informs the hapless Owen as he frogmarches him out of the room.

'Look, maybe I was a bit hasty back there…'

'Too late, Owen, I'm afraid. I've had a lot of stick from the Boss over you; he thinks I've been far too lenient.' Sebastian consults his watch. 'Said, if it wasn't sorted by the end of today, he was calling in your papers.'

'You mean…?'

'That's right. He's terminating your contract.'

Owen feels a tightening in his chest and he finds it hard to breathe. 'Terminating it? But doesn't that involve…dying?'

Sebastian throws an arm around Owen's shoulder. 'No, of course not,' he assures him. 'Don't be so melodramatic.' He gives Owen an affectionate squeeze. 'Well yes, actually it does. But don't worry; I'll make sure it's painless. I've grown quite fond of you, you know.' Owen looks doubtful. 'No, really. But it doesn't do to get emotionally involved with the clients. It clouds the judgement.'

'But couldn't we fake it. Put your watch back an hour?' pleads Owen, who is beginning to regret having been quite so soft where Agnes is concerned.

Sebastian heaves a sigh of regret. 'I'd like to, Owen, you know I would, but it's more than my job's worth, old love. I'm in enough trouble as it is. The Boss just won't tolerate failure. Thanks to this little fiasco, I could be spending the next thousand years listening to Marilyn Monroe singing 'happy birthday Mr President', whilst having a lava enema. Sorry, but that's the way it is. He who must be obeyed has spoken.'

'What about Avril?' Owen asks in a very small voice.

'Ditto. Two birds with one stone, as they say. I did try to help you; lust just isn't your strong suite, unfortunately. Perhaps we should have gone for sloth after all. Still, it's easy to be wise after the event, isn't it?'

'You're saying, that's it; kindly leave the stage. Strut and fret your hour no more?'

'Ah, Macbeth!' muses Sebastian, 'Won-derful play.

Sex and death; always goes down well. Yes, I'm afraid so. The time has come to say, "out, out, brief candle".'

8: AN EXPENSIVE PLACE TO DIE

It's a perfect summer's day. The sun has got his hat on. The sky is an azure blue and matches the colour of the water in the blue-tiled swimming pool. Clad in a skimpy yellow bikini that reveals more than it hides, Avril's shapely limbs are decorously draped over a sun lounger. She is an object of desire for the male guests staying at this luxury hotel on the south coast, who are drawn to her like bees to a honeycomb. Their wives, on the other hand, pay little attention to her male companion; Owen in shorts and 'T' shirt is slouched in a poolside chair. He is nursing a hangover and a long, tall glass of some exotic booze.

Avril pours sun tan lotion onto her arms and chest; begins rubbing it into her skin with long, sensuous strokes. All around the pool, male eyes swivel in her direction; grown men drool. Seemingly oblivious to all this attention, she turns to her companion. 'It was good of Sebastian to let us have this last weekend together,' she says.

'Oh yeah,' Owen says bitterly, 'The condemned couple ate a full English breakfast.'

'Come on, you have to admit it's a nice hotel.'

'It's an expensive place to die, that's all.'

'You're not the only one wishing they were somewhere else, you know.'

Owen fishes the tiny umbrella from out of his drink and tosses it into the pool. He'd almost choked on it. 'Well, what did you expect me to say? Hey, what a nice hotel. Makes a great place to die!'

'You haven't said a word all morning. I was simply trying to make conversation.'

They lapse into a moody silence; Owen staring into his glass, while Avril gazes down into the clear blue water of the pool.

'Why does it have to be with Agnes, anyway? We could make this a dirty weekend. Sebastian could backdate it and we'd be off the hook,' she proposes eagerly. 'Give a whole new meaning to post coital!'

'I've already suggested that. He can't do it.'

'Why on earth not?'

'More than his job's worth, apparently.' Owen sighs. 'Anyway, what's the point? I'll only be back here in another thirty years. What's thirty years compared to eternity? Might as well get it done and over with. There's nothing I'm particularly looking forward to anyway.'

Avril sits up, swings her legs over the side of the lounger and leans forward. Keeping her voice low so that the other guests won't hear, she says, 'You make it sound like there's a dull weekend coming up on the tele or something. Owen, this is the rest of our lives we're talking about here. You can be such a selfish sod sometimes!' she rasps.

Owen sets his glass down by the side of his chair.

'Me?' he says, much louder than he intended and several heads swivel in their direction.

'Keep your voice down,' she hisses. 'Yes, you Owen. You might not have much to live for but I do; his name's Harry and I love him more than I ever thought it was possible to love anyone. I don't understand why I'm here.' Her bottom lip begins to tremble and Owen wonders if there are tears forming behind her dark glasses. 'You're the one who broke his contract. Why is Sebastian making me take the blame?'

Owen is stung by Avril's words. He has not forgotten about her son and he can only imagine the agonies she is going through right now. 'To cover his arse, I expect. He was pissed when he turned up at Agnes's flat. She heard him fall out of the wardrobe. Put the wind up her, I can tell you.' Owen relates the whole sorry tale. 'I just couldn't do it after that. It would have been rape. The poor woman was terrified.'

Avril is silent for a moment. She sits with her head cradled in her hands. 'Oh God, Owen, what are we going to do?' she says despairingly.

'I'm not paying the bloody bill for a start! Have you seen how much they charge here for an evening meal?'

'Christ, Owen, what do you care? You can't take it with you. Jesus!'

'No, but I can leave it to somebody…'

'Leave it to somebody! Who in the wide world could *you* leave it to?'

'I don't know, haven't decided. Needs thinking about.'

Avril manages a smile despite the prevailing gloom. Gallows humour they call it, don't they? 'Well, it won't take long, will it? So, Mr Billy-no-mates, which of your numerous friends and acquaintances is going to be the lucky beneficiary of your little nest egg, then?'

'It might not be much, but at least I worked for it,' he says proudly.

'How very working class of you. Here lies Owen Leadbeater; an honest labourer who earned his salt,' she intones solemnly. 'And I suppose people like me don't work. You try dancing naked for hours at a time in some grotty little club. You earn your money, believe me.'

'Oh sure,' Owen sneers. 'Must be really hard work jigging your arse about and having blokes stuff tenners up your G-string.'

Avril removes her sunglasses, holds them in her lap. 'It's no use trying to talk to you. You're so blinkered you should be pulling a barge!'

'What…?'

'It's a metaphor, Owen. Some people live in the fast lane, but you're not even on the motorway. You're stuck on the towpath; a shire horse; slow, plodding and blinkered!'

'I wasn't always a sad git, you know. I had a life once. Not much of one, I admit, but not so very different from millions of others. I had a job, a wife and a mortgage…I had a future. I just lost it, you know, when Maureen walked out and they made me redundant. I couldn't get my head around it. Everything that made me who I was, just slipping through my fingers like that; turning to dust in my hand. They didn't just take my job – they took away my identity. Overnight I became a non-person. I couldn't handle it; had some kind of breakdown. Afterwards, I could never quite put the pieces back together again. I mean, Owen Leadbeater isn't a job. Owen Leadbeater isn't just one half of somebody else. He is a person in his own right, isn't he?'

Avril reaches out and takes his hand. 'Yes, Owen, he is. We all are. We just find it easier to stick a label on each other so we don't have to look behind the masks we're all wearing.'

'Yours hasn't slipped yet, I notice. So come on, what's your story?'

Avril allows herself a wan smile. 'It's too sad a tale for a sunny day like this, and we don't need to feel any sorrier for ourselves than we do already.'

'You mean, you're not going to tell me?' Owen feels badly let down by Avril's reluctance to share her secrets with him. He has opened his heart to her – they're facing death together – what possible reason can she have now for not sharing her story with him?

Suddenly he is gripped by an urgent desire to get away; shut himself off from these troubling emotions and this crippling sense of impending doom. Leaping from his chair, he dives headfirst into the pool. As the water closes over his head, a feeling of peace and tranquillity comes over him. In this silent world he is weightless and everything is the colour of the sky. He has no sense of up or down; the walls, the floor, the ceiling of his new home are all blue. Owen wants to stay here forever and wonders how long he can hold his breath. If only he had gills instead of lungs, he need never return to that other world. He has heard it said – by those who haven't drowned – that it was one of the more pleasant ways to go. Owen wonders if it's true. He has only to open his mouth to find out – why wait for Sebastian to come and put an end to his miserable little life? If he opens his mouth now, he can stay here forever.

Slowly, tentatively, Owen parts his lips and releases the air from his lungs. He watches enraptured as the stream of bubbles goes rushing to the surface, eager to regain the world of air and of breathing things. The last of the air gone, Owen swallows his first mouthful of chlorinated water and chokes on it. As panic sets in, he discovers, like many a drowning man before him, that it's not such a pleasant way to go after all. His lungs rapidly filling with water, he begins sinking towards the bottom of the pool. The bright, blue world he was so keen to inhabit has suddenly taken on a far darker hue. Arms flailing, he tries to claw his way back to the surface but, despite his frantic efforts, he continues to sink downwards. He hears a detonation above him. There is an explosion of bubbles, a flash of yellow costume, then Owen is gripped under the armpits and carried swiftly upwards. His head breaks the surface and, coughing and spluttering, he takes a greedy gulp of life-giving air.

All around the edge of the pool the other guests, particularly the menfolk, are jostling with each other for the best view. It's not the hapless Owen they are craning their necks to see, however, but Avril. There's a splash to Owen's left as one of the men loses his balance and falls in. The other men simply ignore him; their eyes riveted on the sight of Avril's naked breasts bobbing up and down as she treads water. She turns Owen over onto his back and, cupping a hand under his chin, swims with him to the nearest ladder. Eager hands reach out to help Owen up and onto the poolside. Looking like a Greek goddess, her skin glistening in the sunlight, Avril emerges from the pool to great applause. She accepts it gracefully, though she can't help feeling that she is being applauded more for her impromptu striptease than for rescuing Owen. As she reaches the top of the ladder, she is met by the importunate man who fell into the pool during the frenzied jockeying for a better vantage point. Grinning like a fool, he makes the most of presenting her with the errant bikini top. He then offers his cheek for a kiss and, realising she has nothing much to lose by doing so, she pushes him back in again, to hysterical laughter from his friends. One of the hotel's staff collects their towels and drapes them around their shoulders. Though young, the girl has a calm, self-assured manner and in an authoritative voice requests that the onlookers give the pair some space. Ushering them away to a quiet corner, she identifies herself as Malina Pawlak, assistant under-manager, and asks if she should call for an ambulance or a doctor. Owen assures her that he doesn't need either, just wants to get out of his wet things. Bathrobes are brought to them and accompanied by Malina, he and Avril make their way back to their rooms. As they enter the poolside bar, the room falls silent and Avril receives some dirty looks from her admirers' wives and girlfriends as they pass through on their way to the staircase; an imposing affair of mahogany and marble that is very much in keeping with the rest of the five star hotel's grandiose style.

When the trio reach the door to Owen's room, Malina hands him a business card. 'Call me pleeze, if you change your mind about the doctor,' she says coolly, 'Now, I leave you to get out of your vet thingze.' She is being very polite and professional about it, but this is a damage limitation exercise and her disapproval, though unvoiced, is all too evident.

Avril is seething with rage as she watches Malina step off briskly down the corridor. Once she is out of sight, Owen is going to get both barrels. Blissfully unaware of Avril's anger, he is struggling to unlock his door using the fiddly electronic strip that, since his last stay in a hotel, has usurped the much simpler key. Owen's patience, by now as thin as the stubborn strip of plastic, is on the verge of calling Malina back when, with a soft click, the door opens and he steps inside. Owen's about to close it when Avril gives the door a hefty shove from the other side and sends him flying backwards across the room. Before he can get back up again, she has closed the door and is kneeling astride him; holding him down.

'What the hell was that?' she yells at him. 'I thought we were in this together!'

'What do you mean?' says Owen defensively. 'I just dived in to cool off.'

'No you didn't. You shouldn't tell lies, Owen, you're really bad at it. When you've had as many men lie to you as I have, you can spot 'em a mile off.' She releases him and standing up, walks over to the room's mini bar. Taking out a miniature bottle of brandy and a ready mixed gin and tonic, she hands the brandy and a glass to Owen. 'Here, drink this,' she says, 'Hopefully it will loosen your tongue. Then you can tell me what was really going on in the pool.'

Owen sits up and hugging his knees, says, 'You could at least let me get out of these wet clothes first.'

'Be my guest,' she says, emptying her gin and tonic into a tumbler.

'No, I meant...'

'Forget it, I'm not going anywhere. If you're too shy to change in front of me, you can use the en-suite.'

Owen takes a large, fortifying swig of brandy but it goes down the wrong way and he chokes. 'You needn't worry,' he says hoarsely, 'I won't be pulling a stunt like that again in a hurry.' He hands Avril the empty brandy glass. 'Give me a hand here, will you?' he says.

Avril puts the glass down and helps Owen to his feet. He feels light-headed, woozy; the room spins. He takes a step and staggers. 'Are you alright?' he hears her ask, but her voice sounds muted as if it's coming from a long way off. He squeezes his eyes shut and, when he opens them again a few seconds later, the room has stopped spinning. The brandy hits his system and his head clears a little. 'I'll be alright now,' he assures her. She fetches some dry things for him and he limps off to get showered and changed.

With Owen in the shower, Avril calms down a little and pours herself another drink. How ironic, she muses, Owen has just tried to drown himself and now I'm trying to drown my sorrows. There wasn't that much difference between the two; drinking yourself to death just took longer. She drifts over to the window and gazes out. Below, excited children are noisily splashing about in the pool, while their parents look on from the comfort of a sun lounger and sip their over-priced booze. The rest of the world, it would seem, has moved on. Was that their fate when the end came – to be forgotten by all but those closest to them? She could feel another gin and tonic coming on...

Twenty minutes and a third gin and tonic later, Owen emerges from the bathroom, dressed in dark blue shorts and a pale blue 'T' shirt. He is carrying a towel and he begins vigorously rubbing his hair with it.

'You've been in there a long time,' says Avril. 'I was beginning to think…'

Owen abruptly stops towelling his hair, 'What?' he snaps, 'You were beginning to think what – that I'd drowned myself under the shower or…or slit my wrists with my nail-clippers?'

'No, of course not…but you have a razor, don't you?'

'It's an electric razor,' he informs her scornfully.

Avril raises her hands in surrender. 'Alright… alright, I was being stupid.'

Owen dumps the damp towel. 'No, come here.' he says and, folding his arms around her, hugs Avril to him. 'It's me who has been stupid,' he tells her with a catch in his voice. He can feel her wet costume dampening his dry clothes but is reluctant to let go of her; this is almost certainly the last woman he will ever hold, and he is determined to make the most of it. If only Ashley could see him now; shacked up in a five star hotel with a bikini clad, exotic dancer; the kind of woman wet dreams are made of. In the circumstances, Owen can't help being stirred by these reflections himself and, his arousal threatening to embarrass him, breaks away to perch uncomfortably on the edge of the bed.

'I don't know what came over me,' he begins, after a thoughtful silence. 'When we were down by the pool, I mean…' he adds to avoid any confusion. 'I just had to get away.'

'From me?' asks Avril.

'From everything,' he says abjectly. 'Haven't you ever

felt like that?'

'Yes, once or twice.'

'And what did you do?'

'I booked a holiday… ' Her expression is deadpan. There's a beat and they both fall about laughing. More gallows humour but it breaks the tension that has been building up between them. Though when the laughter subsides, they fall into awkward silence again. It's been a day of silences, reflects Avril; Owen's right – what's the point of staying silent any longer? Having made the decision, she decides the best course of action is to come straight out with it. 'My dad killed himself. That's why I was so angry with you just now.'

Avril's unexpected revelation carries the sting of a whiplash and Owen winces. Sorry has always struck him as a totally inadequate response to this kind of news, but he trots it out anyway. 'I'd no idea,' he adds lamely. It hardly excuses his actions. Still, he blunders on. 'How old were you when he…?'

'Eight, coming up to nine,' the girl says flatly.

'You were old enough to remember him, then.'

'Seems like yesterday sometimes, dad sneaking up to my room with some biscuits after mum sent me off to bed without any supper.'

'Ah, so you've always been a naughty girl.'

'Not really. Mum was very strict, that's all. She wore the trousers in our house. Had to, dad was such a softie. We'd have run rings round him if she hadn't been around to enforce a bit of discipline. He couldn't bear to see us cry, you see.'

'We…?'

'My older brother and me.'

'And where is he now?'

'With dad.'

'Oh, I see.'

'No, I don't think you do. Alan was born with cystic fibrosis. He died when he was twelve. The heart seemed to go out of dad after that. He was a doctor you see; a doctor who couldn't save his own son. Hard to live with that kind of failure.'

'I'm sorry.' That word again. It was fast becoming the word for the day. 'So why did you decide to follow him into the medical profession and become a psychiatrist?'

'I needed to understand what makes people do something like that. Sacrifice themselves in that way.'

'I can understand that, but the lap dancing – what's that all about?'

'They were closing down psychiatric hospitals, putting patients back into the community. There were dozens of us chasing every post. I had no money. I had to do something. A friend of mine was going for an audition at this club and said why don't you come along, it'll be a laugh. So I did. I got the job and lost a friend. Been there ever since.'

'Shame. Doctor Avril Oliver MD has a certain ring to it.' Avril laughs. 'What's so funny?' he asks.

'Silly, Avril Oliver is my stage name. My real name…' she checks herself. 'Never mind, it doesn't matter.'

'No, go on…'

'Promise you won't laugh then,' she says, earnestly.

'Course I won't.'

'You will. Everybody does.'

Owen swings his arm up in a scout's two finger salute. 'Scout's honour,' he vows.

'I bet you were never in the scouts.'

'I was, you know. I'll let you see my woggle, if you like.'

'I've already seen it, remember?'

'No, I didn't mean...'

Owen is still giving her that ridiculous salute. Avril takes hold of his arm and pulls it down to his side. 'It's okay, just cross your heart and hope to... No, never mind,' she says quickly. 'I'll just have to take your word for it. Ready?' Owen nods his head. 'My real name is...' she hesitates, then lets it out in a rush, 'Alison Pig.' She stands back expecting the customary laughter and ribald remarks, but Owen, it seems, is a little more mature than most.

'Pig? Well, there's nothing wrong with... Really... A. Pig?' He clamps his lips tightly together, tries to hold back the laughter that is building up inside him with the irresistible pressure of an oil well about to gush.

'Owen, you promised,' Avril cries when the thin, red line breaks.

'I'm sorry,' he says, his shoulders heaving, 'but with a name like that you should have been a vet!'

'So much for scout's honour,' she says, and tosses her gin and tonic, complete with lemon slice, at him. From less than half a metre away she can't miss and it hits Owen squarely between the eyes.

'Feel better for having a good laugh, do you?'

'Yeah, I do actually, I feel a lot better. Do you want another drink?'

'I'm okay thanks, I'll just lick that one off your face.'

'Oh, very dry.'

'Unlike your face,' she says with a sweet smile.

Owen retrieves the towel he discarded earlier and

wipes at his sticky, wet face. When he lowers the towel, the errant lemon slice falls out of its folds and plops onto the carpet. He scoops it up and drops it into the waste bin. Straightening up he says, 'I bet Sebastian laughed when you told him your name was Pig.'

'We were at the club. I used my stage name.'

'Avril Oliver... why?'

'Wouldn't you, if your name was Pig?'

'No, it was a legal document. You should have used your real name.'

'I doubt if it makes any difference to Sebastian what I call myself.'

'But it does, don't you see? Sebastian has a contract with Avril Oliver, not you.' A sudden thought occurs to him. 'Unless, you changed your name by deed poll... please tell me you didn't. It is still Pig not Oliver, isn't it?'

Avril, or should he now call her Alison, still looks doubtful, 'Yes, but are you sure you've got this right?'

'Look at it this way,' says Owen with some impatience. 'If you had signed it as Minnie Mouse, do you think that contract would still be legal? I'm telling you, you're off the hook. That contract isn't worth the paper it's written on. You can tell Sebastian to stick it where the sun doesn't shine!'

Avril still can't quite believe it, 'Oh Owen, really?' He nods his head emphatically and her face lights up. 'But that's wonderful. We're saved. We're saved!' It feels like they've won the lottery. In their new-found joy they hug and kiss, and hug and kiss again, then slowly drawing apart, hold one another at arm's length; look at each other in amazement. 'Come on, let's get out of here,' says Avril and starts tugging him towards the door. But Owen holds her back. 'Owen, come on, what are you waiting for?'

'Hell to freeze over?' he says bleakly, 'Unlike you, I've still got a one-way ticket.'

'You're not Mickey Mouse?'

'No, I wasn't as smart as you. I was stupid enough to let Sebastian sign me up in my real name. Can you believe it? Oh shit, shit, shit, shit! My surname should have been Pratt!'

'Owen, don't; if we hadn't been in the Club, I would have used my real name too.' She pulls him into her arms; kisses him lightly on the lips. Lips that still retain the bitter/sweet taste of gin. She kisses him again, this time more firmly and Owen responds in kind. He matches her kiss for kiss as their passion grows. Her tongue finds his and Owen is reaching for the clasp of her bikini top when Sebastian slips inside the door and announces his presence with a half-hearted round of applause. The amorous couple are so startled they almost jump apart.

'Ah, ain't love grand,' Sebastian scoffs, 'So glad to see you two getting on so famously.' He crosses to the min-bar and helps himself to a drink.

Owen steps forward manfully, 'Sebastian, I think you should know,' he says earnestly, 'that there's been a development…'

But Avril cuts him short. 'Not now, Owen.'

'So I see,' observes Sebastian drily, whilst settling himself into a comfortable chair. 'While the cat's away, eh? Well, fill me in. I want to hear all the sordid details; who did what to whom and where.'

'It's not how it looks…'

'Au contraire, my dear Owen; a blind man could see what's going on here. Such *passion*, I knew you had it in you, deep down. Of course I hadn't realised just how deep we'd have to trawl, but we managed to stir those still waters of yours in the end. So gratifying to see one's plan come to such a fruitful conclusion.'

'Plan? What are you talking about?'

'Why, my simple but ingenious little plan, to get you and the lovely Avril into the same bed of course! I knew that in a life or death situation you'd do what most human beings do on these occasions and take one last gallop round the park, as it were.'

'What… you mean this was a set-up? You let us think we were going to die tomorrow just to put the two of us in the right frame of mind for a shag?' Owen is incensed by this heartless deception. 'Have you any idea what we've been through this weekend, thanks to your so called master plan?'

Avril pulls him away. 'Don't waste your breath Owen, he'd have to have a heart to care.'

'Still, it was unnecessarily cruel, even for him,' Owen observes bitterly.

Sebastian treats him to a disdainful smile, 'Sometimes you have to be cruel to be kind,' he says, and takes his drink over to the window. 'Umm, lovely view… ' He takes an appreciative sip of a crisp Pinot Grigio.

'So…, does this mean we're off the hook?' Owen asks.

'That depends…' Sebastian replies without turning around.

'On what?'

'On whether you and the *lady*…' he says this with a faint but unmistakable sneer, 'know each other in the biblical sense or not.' He brings those penetrating eyes of his to bear on them. 'Well…?'

Knowing that Owen will only damn himself, Avril steps in front of her would be lover and squares up to Sebastian. 'We would have done, if you hadn't come barging in on us like that!'

'Don't listen to her. She's only saying that to save me.'

'From what exactly?'

'Myself…'

'Oh, come off it, Owen, there's no need to be coy. You were well up for it, you know you were.' Then to Sebastian, 'Another few minutes and you would have caught us *in flagrante.*'

Sebastian's finely chiselled features are split by a broad grin. 'Owen, I salute you!' He holds his wine glass aloft. 'The shire horse has become a stallion.' He turns to Avril, 'Can I have him when you've finished with him?'

'You'll have to join the queue, we could be some time. Come on, Owen darling, let's go to my room,' she says, and taking him by the hand, endeavours to lead him to the door.

But Owen steadfastly refuses to move 'No, tell him Avril.' His companion, her face a picture of dejection, shakes her head. 'Alright then, I will.'

'Tell me what?'

'Her name isn't Avril Oliver, it's Alison Pig.'

'Oh Owen…'

'So what if it is?'

'You're one soul short matey, that's what. The contract she signed is null and void. You understand me? Not legally binding. She has a built-in get-out clause.'

For once Sebastian's cultivated air of cool

detachment deserts him and he appears unsure of himself. 'Well, I'll have to study the small print of course, but *if* what he says is true... you used a pseudonym?'

'My stage name, yes.'

'I don't see how we could have overlooked it. We're always so careful about that sort of thing, especially when dealing with authors and theatricals.'

But Owen is as tenacious as a dog with a bone as he pursues the point. 'Be that as it may,' he presses, 'she is free to go – right?'

'On the face of it, it would seem so,' Sebastian reluctantly agrees.

'Go on then Av... Alison, off you go.'

'I'm not going without you,' she says firmly and gives Owen's hand a squeeze.

Sebastian is quick to seize the opening, 'Yes, let's not be too hasty...' he says.

'No. You slipped up on this one, now leave her A-LONE!'

Sebastian, who up to this point has viewed Avril as a useful ally, sees that she has become more of a hindrance than an asset; her presence only serving to encourage Owen's pathetic display of macho posturing. He's seen it all before, of course; the human male ego out to impress the female of the species with one last bold huzzah before they go. 'My dear, would you excuse us for a moment. I'd like a quiet word with Owen, if you don't mind.'

'I'd prefer to stay...'

'You heard him,' says Owen. 'Now please, go and pack.' He raises the girl's hand to his lips and kisses it. She looks hurt and, silently mouthing he is sorry, he gives her a gentle push towards the door; receiving one last sad-eyed look before she closes the door behind her.

'This is very noble of you Owen, but why? Why make this grand gesture for someone you barely know? A case of *"It is a far, far better thing that I do, than I have ever done,"* is that it?'

'I just don't see the point of dragging her down with me, that's all. She's got a second chance, she should take it. Nothing very noble in that.'

'And you think she would do the same for you?'

'Yes, of course.' Sebastian gives him a sideways look. 'Well you heard her just now. It wasn't just her own skin she was trying to save.'

'She knew you wouldn't take her up on it,' he growls. 'It was little more than a gesture, and an empty one at that.'

'That's a matter of opinion.'

'It's a fact, little man,' says Sebastian nastily, his anger growing. 'I know human nature, I should do, I've studied it long enough. Five hundred years of collecting souls has taught me one thing about you lot...'

'And what's that?'

'You're all so fucking predictable.' He pours himself another glass of wine. 'So predictable, it bores the arse off me. So you see, Owen, hell for me is being here.'

'Sorry to have disappointed you...'

'Don't sell yourself short, Owen. There are exceptions to every rule; the occasional square peg, as it were.'

'And that's how you see me, is it – a square peg in a round hole?'

'Oh, don't be so modest, Owen; you're not just a square, you're a polygon... a decahedron!'

'I'm just being myself. I'm too old and set in my ways to change.'

'Nonsense, you're in your prime! And you've still got thirty-two years left to enjoy the best that life has to offer. Come with me, Owen, there's someone I want you to meet...'

*

They are in one of London's smartest hotels; the kind of place Owen couldn't afford to eat lunch, let alone stay in. A coldly polite, well-built man in a nicely tailored lounge suit has just asked to see their invitations. Owen is amazed when, in response, Sebastian nonchalantly reaches into an inside pocket and produces some. The security man examines them carefully then waves them through.

The room they enter resembles a small lecture theatre. The decor is wall-to-wall blue; plush, dark blue carpeting, pale blue walls and rows of cinema-style, mid-blue seating with gangways down the middle and on both sides. In front of some dark blue drapes is a raised area, in the centre of which two swivel chairs and a low table have been set up. On the table there is a selection of mineral waters and two tall glasses. Scattered around the room, a bunch of bleary-eyed hacks are doing their best to look bored, whilst down by the stage their accompanying photographers swap stories of how they 'papped' this or that celeb. There are several television news crews too and an over-coiffured female reporter from Sky News speaks into a microphone while her sound man checks his levels.

Few of the hacks bother to look up from their iPhones when a young woman in a dark suit, her hair scraped back from her forehead into a severe bun, enters from a side room and introduces herself. She boasts a double-barrelled name and is from the PR company responsible for organising this press conference. She sounds as though she is giving an elocution lesson as she proceeds to outline the ground rules for putting questions to the 'A' list actor, whose imminent arrival centre stage is heralded by the life-sized cut-outs of him which stand either side of a blow-up of the poster for his latest action movie. Owen, who has several of the star's films on DVD at home, is excited at the prospect of seeing him in the flesh. Observing his companion's growing excitement, Sebastian is encouraged to believe he may yet bag both souls and redeem himself in the eyes of his master.

The spokeswoman from the PR company welcomes the leading man and his love interest in the movie – a newcomer to the big screen – onto the stage, then steps to one side. Owen is struck by how much smaller than his celluloid self the 'A' Lister is in person; ironic really, as he is reputed to have an ego big enough to fill an entire solar system. The pair settle themselves into the swivel chairs and the action-man star pours a glass of mineral water for himself and his attractive companion; a Hitchcock blonde in a tight sweater and skinny jeans. The room is suddenly bathed in the cold, blue light of electronic flash as the photographers begin snapping away; their cameras' motor drives sounding like a chorus of singing mice. There is a slightly nervous exchange of banter between the star and the journos at the start of the interview, but his dazzling Hollywood smile and his easy-going charm is hard to resist and the girl is a looker, if a trifle star-struck...

Owen turns to Sebastian who, judging by the rapt

expression on his face, is similarly stricken and says, 'So, why are we here exactly?'

'Ummm...' For a moment it seems that Sebastian hasn't heard the question, so entranced is he by the handsome actor. Owen is about to repeat it when Sebastian, without shifting his gaze replies, 'I wanted you to see just what your noble gesture is going to cost you.' Then tearing himself away, he takes Owen's arm and draws him to the rear of the room. He points at the actor who is explaining how he prepared for his latest role; in the process making some dubious connections with the character's back story and his own early life. 'That could be you down there,' he tells Owen.

'Yeah right,' Owen snorts. 'It would take a million dollars' worth of cosmetic surgery to make me look like him!'

'I don't mean him per se; someone *like* him. Really, Owen, you can be irritatingly pedantic at times. You can choose to be anything you like – a best-selling author perhaps, or an entrepreneur and grow rich beyond your wildest dreams; have a car for each day of the week and a different woman every night. Owen, you can have anything or anyone you want; be sensible, don't make netting you so easy for me. You're on the road to hell anyway – why not take the scenic route?'

'You're asking me to change the habits of a lifetime; be something that I'm not.'

'You'd like to rub Ashley's nose in it, wouldn't you?' says Sebastian slyly.

'Ashley?'

'Your, oh so successful younger brother... remember?'

'I know who he is.'

'Picture it, Owen, You could buy a magnificent mansion set in acres of parkland,' he sweeps his arm out in a wide arc. 'Own everything for as far as you can see. You invite your brother and his wife down for a weekend in the country; give them a conducted tour guaranteed to take their breath away; day rooms, bedrooms, galleries stuffed with antiques and objets d'art from all over the world. Come on Owen, MONEY, SEX and REVENGE… it's an irresistible combination.'

'It wouldn't work. He'd know.'

'Who would know what?'

'My brother… he'd know I wasn't capable of being a best-selling author, whatnot.'

'We wouldn't do it overnight. We'd build you up over a period of years. I mean, we didn't let a corporal invade Poland, did we?'

'Poland? You mean…'

'Precisely. Between you and me, things got a bit out of hand there.'

'I'll say.'

'All the little man wanted was to be a famous artist. The local art college snubbed him, apparently. An inexperienced colleague got his German a bit muddled. Told him he could have *everything*, when he meant to say anything. *Alles* instead of *irgend etwas*. A subtle difference, I know, but it's important to get these things right. I should steer clear of world domination if I were you; the Boss does rather look upon that as his domain these days.'

'Fair enough, but I could be Lord of the Manor, right?'

'Lord of the Manor, Knight of the Garter…'

'Really, Sir Owen? I like the sound of that.' He pictures himself kneeling before the Queen at Buckingham Palace. 'I can just see Ashley's face as the Queen taps me on the shoulder with the flat of her sword and says, 'Arise Sir Owen Leadbeater'.'

'A knight wouldst need a fair lady… Lady Avril has a certain ring to it, don't you think?'

'Oh, you bastard!' Heads turn and people glare at them. Owen drops his voice to a rasping whisper. 'You almost had me hooked there. I can't believe I fell for it. You just want me to help you reel Avril in. Well, no way. I've told you, I'm not betraying her.'

'Oh dear, love rears its ugly head again I fear.'

'I'm not in love with her,' Owen insists.

'Of course you're not. When will you ever learn, Owen? What has this love nonsense ever brought you other than unhappiness and betrayal? You don't deny it, I notice,' he adds when Owen doesn't contradict him.

'I don't need to. I'm fond of her, nothing more.'

'Fond? Looked a lot more than that to me! Fond is a peck on the cheek. Fond is a brotherly hug. Fond isn't trying to remove someone's tonsils with your tongue.'

'Things got a bit emotional, I admit, but I didn't touch her tonsils.'

'Have it your own way but you weren't giving her mouth to mouth resuscitation, were you?' He drops the hectoring tone. 'Look, don't get me wrong, a bit of foreplay is long overdue, but if you want her, you have to be prepared to go all the way.'

'Forget it. The price is too high. I'm kebab meat whatever happens, but I don't have to drop her in the chilli sauce!'

'You won't be dropping her in it; she wants to be with you. It's a price she's prepared to pay. Don't knock it.'

'Why won't you let her be? Does it really matter if you have one soul more or less in hell in thirty years' time? Are you on a bonus or something? Is there a price on our heads?'

'Of course not, but we all have our quotas to fill and the Boss expects us to meet them.'

'Quotas?'

'Yes, quotas. It's a business, Owen. He's a soul trader. I've bent over backwards to help you. Why can't you do this one little thing for me? I'm not asking you to twist the girl's arm, just do what comes naturally. Most men would be up there as quick as a ferret up a trouser-leg. Lie back and think of England if you have to, but nail her to the mattress. I can give you to the end of the week, after that it's out of my hands.'

9: TEQUILA SUNSET

It's a pretty little station, or would be on a sunny day. The fine weather has broken as it always does in England during the summer months, and a fine drizzle of warm rain falls like dew from a leaden sky. In the dull, grey light the bright colours of the bedding plants that decorate the station's borders and tubs seem muted; the colour washed out of their petals as if they have been painted on with watercolour.

This change from major to minor mirrors the mood of the couple sitting on a platform bench; they huddle together, not so much for warmth but for comfort. The observant onlooker would note that only one of them has any luggage. If they were at all interested, they would probably assume that one of them was seeing the other off. Owen stares grim-faced across the tracks to the opposite platform, where a cocky seabird is parading up and down as if he owns it. Another wheels overhead; first a Hitchcock blonde and now Hitchcock's birds have come to feed on his carcass.

'How long?' Avril asks; she is the first to break a silence that has lasted for a full ten minutes now.

Owen lifts a Styrofoam cup of coffee to his lips and takes a sip. 'He didn't say.'

Avril gives an involuntary shudder. 'I hate this waiting; goodbyes are best kept brief. Dragging them out just makes it all the more painful.'

Owen gives her a wan smile. 'You ever see Brief Encounter?' he asks. Avril's blank expression says she hasn't. 'It's an old black and white film about this couple who meet and fall in love in a railway station. They're both married; he's a doctor and she's a bored suburban housewife…'

'And they have a passionate affair?'

'Sort of – they're very British and stiff upper lip about it – and even when one of the doctor's friends agrees to let them use his place to consummate their lust, it all goes wrong when he comes home early and interrupts them. That's when they realise it's impossible to carry on seeing each other and decide to end the affair. They arrange to meet one last time in the railway station tearoom, but once again they're interrupted, when the woman's talkative friend turns up and won't leave them alone. So they never get the chance to say goodbye properly, and have to make do with shaking hands…'

'I prefer happy endings myself,' says Avril with some feeling.

Owen claps his hands together intending to scare the gull away, but succeeds only in making Avril jump. The defiant bird, meanwhile, continues to patrol platform one with the jaunty air of a sailor. 'That's because you're an optimist,' says Owen, glowering at the gull and wishing he had a gun. 'The truth is there was never going to be a happy ending; their fate was sealed from the start.'

'You're not just talking about the film now, are you?'

'You have to admit there are certain parallel's…' Owen anxiously consults his watch. 'Where the hell is he?'

Avril voices what they are both thinking. 'Hit the nail on the head there, I'd say,' she says.

'Yeah, pound to a penny he's down there right now preparing the chilli dip.'

'I'm sorry?'

'Private joke. Sebastian's a big kebab fan; likes his meat hot and spicy.'

'I'll bet he does,' says Avril archly.

Owen swallows the last of his coffee. 'Well, it takes all sorts, I suppose. And he's not a bad sort really – for a devil, that is. He did give me extra time when he could have blown the final whistle on me weeks ago. But that's the trouble with us old squares, we keep getting stuck in round holes.'

'You're not old and you don't have to be to feel out of place. I've never really fitted in either. We're a couple of misfits, that's what we are.' She gives him an affectionate squeeze.

'You're not old. You're young and you're beautiful – come on – you know you are. You could have any man you wanted. Why haven't you married a millionaire?'

'I've been waiting for Sebastian to turn you into one,' she says and smiles.

'Course you have. Seriously though, why haven't you?'

'Millionaires don't marry girls like me…'

'What, beautiful girls with PhDs?'

'No, exotic dancers with a kid.'

'You should go for one of the older guys – the older the better really – then you could shag him to death and inherit his millions.'

'Owen, stop it.'

'What?'

'You know what. This silly game you're playing. It's all very clever but you're missing the point.'

'The point? Huh, there is no fucking point!' says Owen hotly.

'Listen to me, *please*. I know you're just trying to put on a brave face, but you don't have to. Not for me. Sebastian's the one who likes playing games – save it for him. Look at me, Owen,' she pulls his face towards her. 'You're afraid and I'm afraid for you. Who wouldn't be? So, don't waste whatever time we have left together putting on an act. Don't go all stiff upper lip on me like that doctor and his housewife. There's nothing wrong with being yourself. You're an honest man, a decent man and one of the nicest guys I've ever met.'

'Yes, and you know what they say about nice guys, don't you?'

'What's that?'

'They always come last.'

'Last, but not least…' She takes his face in her hands, kisses him on the forehead and then on the mouth.

The afternoon drags on and with no sign of Sebastian; Owen's nerves are stretched almost to breaking point. 'Damn him, he's taking his time.'

'Maybe he's not coming,' says Avril, who has begun to hope that the fallen angel's non-appearance is due to a last minute reprieve.

'Don't be stupid,' Owen snarls. 'Of course he's coming!' He jumps to his feet. 'Sorry,' he says, and pulling some change from his pocket, walks briskly away.

'Owen… where are you going?' she shouts after him.

'To get another bloody coffee!' he calls back over his shoulder.

*

It stops raining and the clouds begin to thin out. As they slowly drift away, grey sky is gradually replaced by blue and the sun, riding low in the sky, makes a belated appearance. Avril's train comes into sight; not much more than a shapeless blob at first, it could be anything. But soon Owen can make out the cab windows, buffers, wheels. As it pulls into the station he gets to his feet, and picking up Avril's suitcase, carries it to the platform's edge. The doors swing open and holidaymakers laden with bags and cases begin disembarking. Owen glances back towards the bench and is surprised to find Avril hasn't moved. He lugs the case back over to her.

'Come on, this is your train,' he shouts above the hubbub of excited voices and the slamming of doors.

She has been staring into her lap but at his approach, looks up to reveal eyes filled with sorrow. 'I know. I'll catch the next one.'

'But there isn't another one for hours.'

'It doesn't matter. I'm not going anywhere until Sebastian turns up. So you might as well sit down again.'

Owen sits back down, watches numbly as the guard blows his whistle and the train pulls out of the station. Gathering speed, it rumbles down the track and is soon lost in the distance. With the train gone an eerie silence falls over the platform. He and Avril sit there holding hands like an old married couple as the sun completes its arc across the sky and dips towards the horizon. As it sinks, burning gold cools to a glowering red.

'What's the matter?' Avril asks when Owen suddenly grips her hand tightly.

'He's here,' he says quietly.

They turn as one and there standing at the end of the platform, silhouetted in the sun's fiery embers, is Sebastian. He doesn't beckon or call but stands immobile as a statue, immaculate in a dark blue suit. He could be a banker, a businessman, or a civil servant returning home from his day's toil in the city. He looks nothing like the grim reaper of popular mythology with his black robes and a scythe. But then he is a businessman of sorts, a trader in futures; immortal souls for short term earthly gain.

'Run, just run, why don't you?' urges Avril.

'Run...where to? There's no way out of this. It's whatchamacallit... kismet.' He pulls her to her feet. 'You should go now. Go on, there's nothing more you can do here.' Owen takes Avril's tear-streaked face in both hands and kisses her. 'At least we got to say goodbye properly,' he says, then quickly walks away towards the dark figure shimmering in the sunset's glare.

Avril watches transfixed as the two silhouettes come together, seeming to meld into one. Behind them the dying sun suddenly bursts back into life, burning with a light so intense that the watching girl is forced to close her eyes. When she judges it safe to open them again, the sun is a dying ember once more, and the two figures have gone.

GAMES PEOPLE PLAY

TWO SHORT STORIES

BY

CHRIS NIBLOCK

NIGHTS ALONE WITH GARBO

There is a certain time of night; a lonely hour when time itself seems suspended and an eerie stillness descends on deserted streets. With it comes a rare moment of silence. A silence so profound that it's almost a physical thing; a Berlin Wall cutting you off from the rest of your kind, as they lie snug and warm behind the curtains of their darkened bedrooms.

It was that time of night for me, and it was that kind of job – a routine matrimonial case. The usual story: an errant husband, a suspicious wife. That's where I come in, or somebody like me; an insomniac prepared to sit out the wee small hours in a cramped, uncomfortable car. Just sit and watch and wait for something to happen. In three long hours nothing had moved out there – not even a stray cat – since Carlyle and the blonde went in at eleven o'clock. The girl matched the description my client had given me; tall, leggy… the dancer. A nice mover – my description, not my client's – fluid, athletic; the kind of girl who always attracts the wrong kind of men; men like me for instance, or my client's husband.

The girl had only been in view for perhaps thirty seconds; the time it took her to get out of the car and let herself into the flat. Just thirty seconds, but it had been long enough to keep me thinking about her for three hours of watching the hands on the dashboard clock go round, of chain-smoking cigarettes until the pack lay empty on the passenger seat.

It was that time of night when the cigarettes have run out and nothing moves, and nobody's waiting up for you, or even wonders where the hell you are. It's at moments like these that I ask myself why I'm doing this job. When being a private eye seems like a bloody futile way to earn a living. In books and movies there were car chases and gun fights and beautiful women out to seduce the rugged detective.

So, where was the glamour? Where was the excitement in this cold and lonely vigil? I stared across the street at the darkened window on the second floor; tried not to think about the man and the woman up there, but I had my answer. She was in bed with my client's husband – the nice little mover in the red shoes, the fur hat and coat, and nothing on underneath.

It was that time of night. When still air becomes still water to drown in and an empty life is paraded in slow motion before the eyes of drowning men. Grasping at straws, I reached for a cigarette, cursed the empty packet and instead pulled the manila file towards me. Opening it, I angled the pages to catch the light from a street lamp.

The subject's name was Edmund Carlyle,

Conservative MP with a marginal seat in Yorkshire. He was married with three children, all of them daughters. Career, undistinguished so far, but expected to do well. He was currently holding down a junior post at the Health Ministry, as well as numerous directorships on the boards of several well-known companies, and some that were not so well known and registered in the Cayman Islands. Had an honours degree in economics. Owned homes in West Yorkshire and London, along with a holiday home in the South of France – Provence, where else? The flat, however, belonged to the girl. Still, Carlyle was a classic example of the man who had everything.

I turned to the second sheaf of papers in the file. The girlfriend was Lysette Garbo, at least that was her stage name. Real name, Geraldine Dawkins – doesn't have quite the same ring, does it? There was very little else. Unmarried. No children, but one abortion five years ago. No criminal record. There was a newspaper clipping with a photograph of the chorus line from an Andrew Lloyd Webber musical. Lysette was in the back row; happy and smiling in a sequinned outfit and one of those ridiculous plumed head-dresses they wear. The skimpy outfit displayed her figure to its best advantage. It was a wonderful body.

I closed the file; closed my eyes too, but the image of Lysette Garbo wouldn't go away. My eyes were drawn back to the window across the road and I wondered what it would be like with a girl like that. As if on cue the lady herself appeared, muffled in a fur coat and in a hurry. She ran out of the building, jumped into her Citroen and sped off at high speed.

The sudden explosion of sound and the abrupt

change in the landscape caught me off guard for a moment and, although I'd automatically started the car, I hesitated to follow the Citroen. It was Lysette's flat – why was she leaving rather than Carlyle? And why was she in such a hurry to get out of there? I switched off the engine, decided to stay put and wait for Carlyle to make his move. If he was coming out, he'd be down soon. If not, I might have to go up there and take a look. The minutes slowly ticked by and I filled them trying to make one of those Japanese paper sculptures out of the empty cigarette packet. At the end of half an hour, Carlyle still hadn't appeared and I had failed to convert my Benson & Hedges carton into anything like a recognisable shape.

There was nothing for it but to go up to the flat and assess the situation. Taking a torch from the glove compartment, I locked the car and stepped as lightly as I could across the street. Even so, my footsteps sounded like gun shots in the still air. Above my head, Orion's belt hung like an accusing finger in a conscience-clear sky.

I don't know what it was – some innate instinct for smelling out trouble maybe – but suddenly I felt uneasy. Something was very wrong, I felt sure of it. Abandoning caution, I began to run, taking in great gulps of cold air that seared my lungs. I barrelled through the glazed doors. Directly ahead of me was the entrance to the ground floor flat, to my right a flight of concrete steps led up to the first floor and Lysette Garbo's front door. From the outside the two-storey flats had looked quite smart, but here in the stairwell there was a strong smell of tom-cats and a collection of milk bottles, unrinsed and growing green with mould. I checked the torch was working, then took the stairs two at a time. I was aware of making a lot of noise but had the feeling that it no longer mattered.

Lysette's door was open a crack; a narrow beam of yellow light escaping into the hallway. I pressed my ear into the gap and listened. Nothing, just the clink of cooling radiators as the heating shut down. Carlyle wasn't watching TV or listening to the radio. He wasn't washing up or clearing his throat or snoring or padding around the flat in his bare feet. He was either asleep or...

I inched the door open until the gap was wide enough for me to peer through. The door opened onto a small vestibule with a terracotta tiled floor, an umbrella stand with umbrella and a pair of flat-heeled shoes; the kind women wear for driving. There was no sign of Carlyle. I stepped inside the vestibule and, leaving the door slightly ajar for a quick getaway, tip-toed along the hallway.

The first door I came to was the bathroom. Carlyle wasn't taking a bath but somebody had and recently. Soap suds were still visible around the plug and taps. Moonlight filtering through venetian blinds threw a barred pattern onto the still wet porcelain.

Next door was the kitchen; standard fitted cupboards and work-tops along with more terracotta tiles, but no Carlyle.

The lounge was in darkness so I used my torch. I splashed its yellow beam over a three-piece suite that looked brand new; a two-seater Chesterfield with matching arm chairs in rich, dark brown leather. There were Degas prints on the walls; ballerinas and Can-Can dancers and, as I passed the torch-light over them, they seemed to spring to life for a moment; the colours brightening just as when a candle flame flares up when a door is opened, then dies down again.

Something pale and white lay stretched out in front of the Regency-style fireplace – a sheepskin rug – not a body. The lady was obviously into fur in a big way and Carlyle was rich enough to keep her in furs for the rest of her life, or at least for as long as he found her attractive. But where was he? Why had Lysette run out on him?

The answer to these questions was waiting for me in the bedroom. The body was sprawled across the bed, naked but for a pair of black stockings, one of which was knotted around the throat. Lysette Garbo's, not Carlyle's. It must have been Carlyle who had run out to the Citroen in the fur hat and coat. Probably had his trousers rolled up underneath. There was no sign of his clothes but the girl's things were scattered around the room and, like her, they looked crumpled and abandoned. She'd obviously put up a fight. A table lamp had been knocked over; it lay on its side, the light shining out of the narrow top of the shade shone straight into the girl's unseeing eyes. The bed-clothes were scrunched up under her heels as though she had been trying to kick her way out from under her attacker. My guess was that he'd been astride her, pinning her arms down and pulling upwards on the ligature; a kinky game that had got out of hand.

I hadn't seen too many dead bodies in my time, certainly none as beautiful as this girl had been. I stared at the broken doll on the bed and remembered the lithe young dancer who had got out of the car earlier. I'd been captivated by the way she moved, like a big cat or a thoroughbred racehorse. Poetry in motion, as the song goes.

By rights I should have left everything exactly as it

was and called the police immediately. But the case was all sown up – I knew who the killer was and, once I'd informed them, it wouldn't take the police long to pick him up. He was too well known to evade them for any length of time. Meanwhile, it wouldn't hurt to take a few photographs of a murder that was going to put my name on the front page of every newspaper. Sounds callous, especially with the girl lying there, her body not yet cold, but at that moment, I felt strangely elated. Like I'd just won the pools or had a horse come in at 100-1. The tabloids would be falling over themselves to buy my story – it couldn't be better; naked girl found dead, murdered by a well-known MP after kinky sex romp. It was sensational stuff.

Already planning how I would spend the money, I ran down to the car and grabbed my Polaroid camera. Returning to the flat, I photographed the body from several angles; full-length and in close-up. To save time, I didn't wait for each Polaroid to develop before taking the next one, but placed them on the bed as they ejected and just kept shooting until the film ran out. It was a weird sensation watching those ten images in their various stages of development, coming to life before my eyes; comparing them with the original; knowing that the blood was already beginning to congeal in her lifeless veins.

I was blowing on the last of the prints, trying to dry it, when I heard a metallic click in the other room and a bar of light appeared under the door. Someone had switched a light on in the lounge. Had Carlyle returned to the scene of his crime? Heart thumping, I scooped up the Polaroids, slipped them into the inside pocket of my trench coat, and then remembered the camera. Hastily removing the coat, I slung the strap over my shoulder and put the coat back on again. It was a short strap and the camera nestled in my armpit like a concealed weapon. For the first time in my life I found myself wishing I carried a gun.

Taking a deep breath, I gripped the door handle and prepared to make my entrance. If it was Carlyle out there, I was in trouble. There was no way I could walk out of that bedroom and pretend I hadn't seen the body. If it was anyone else, I could probably convince them that I was a friend of Lysette's from the theatre; a fellow dancer perhaps, or a musician. Adopting what I hoped was a theatrical air, I stepped out of the bedroom and closed the door firmly behind me.

The middle-aged woman in evening dress, her throat ringed with pearls, gave a startled cry and dropped the poker she was brandishing.

'Oh, Mr Dawkins,' she fluttered. 'Thank goodness it's you. I thought you'd got burglars!' She stared in surprise at the grubby trench coat and the fedora hat I was wearing. 'Is everything all right? Only the door was open and I thought…'

'Just walked in.' I explained. 'Must have forgotten to close it.' I removed the hat. 'Fancy dress party – I went as Bogart. I gave her a reassuring smile. 'And you?' I enquired pleasantly. 'You look as though you've been somewhere nice.'

'Old girls' reunion; school, you know, chance to catch up with each other's news. Yes, it was very nice to see everyone again…' Her voice trailed off and there was an awkward silence in which Miss Harris appeared to drift off into her own thoughts. I doubted if she'd had much to tell her old school chums; her life seemed pretty empty from what I'd seen of it. 'Well,' she said finally. 'As long as everything's all right here, I'll take myself off to bed. I'm not used to these late nights.'

'Right. Well, I'm sorry you've been troubled, Miss Harris. We haven't been using the town flat much lately, I should have warned you we were coming down.' I was ushering her towards the front door. 'By the way,' I said. 'You didn't call the police or anything, did you?'

Miss Harris put her hands to her face. 'No, no I didn't. I should have though, shouldn't I?'

'Quite right,' I said, oozing sincerity. 'It doesn't do to tackle these young thugs on your own.'

Miss Harris was flattered by my concern. She actually blushed. 'Good night then,' she simpered.

'Night Miss Harris. Sleep well.'

*

'It's a good job she didn't come barging in here,' said Geraldine when I returned to the bedroom. 'She'd have got the shock of her life.' She was sat on the edge of the bed in silk pyjamas now; the black stockings lay discarded at her feet.

I took the Polaroids out and tossed them onto the bed. 'Yes, I must make sure I shut the front door next time.'

'You know some of these photos are rather good,' mused Geraldine as she spread them out on the bed. 'You're getting quite good at it. I'm tired of that name though.'

'What name?'

'Lysette Garbo. I'm always Lysette Garbo when we play these games. Why is that? Is she an ex-girlfriend of yours?'

'No, of course not.'

'So, why the fixation with the name?'

'It's not a fixation. I just think it sounds more glamorous than yours, that's all.'

'Well, think of something else,' snapped Geraldine without looking up. 'I want Lysette Garbo killed off for good.'

*

And I did, about a year later, when I killed Geraldine and Lysette Garbo at one and the same time. I did it for the money of course. Geraldine had lots of it. She gave me a generous allowance but money's always been something I could never get enough of. I did miss our little games for a while, but then, when you have pots of money, you can always find someone to play with. I do regret killing the other girls though, that was unfortunate, but the police always suspect the husband when their wife is murdered, and I had to convince them that Geraldine's murder was not an isolated incident but the work of a serial killer. So, in the months leading up to the murders, I placed a series of adverts featuring some of the Polaroids I'd taken of Geraldine, but under the name of Lysette Garbo, in various contact magazines offering kinky sex to like-minded readers. I picked the other women at random from the pages of the same magazines.

I was of course suitably upset, indeed shocked, to find my wife had been leading this extraordinary double-life. The detectives leading the investigation into my wife's murder were so impressed by my obvious sincerity that I was quickly eliminated from their enquiries. It goes without saying of course, that I also had a cast iron alibi.

That was three years ago and now it's one of those nights when it's too warm to sleep and the surf breaking over the reef below my house is like a heartbeat that pounds a fraction of a second behind my own. One of those nights, like last night and the night before that, when the wind keeps me awake. Howling in the palm trees, it screams out her name.

GAR – BO… GAR – BO.

EMILY ON THE EDGE

Sometimes my patients bring me things. It's usually chocolates or a few flowers. Occasionally, it's a memento from their past; an ornament perhaps, or a faded photograph; a small gift they want me to have or memory they want to share with me.

Emily – it's not her real name – brought me a picture; an exquisite little watercolour in a polished wooden frame, wrapped in hessian and tied up with string. She handed it to me shyly like a schoolgirl bringing an apple to her teacher, then took several steps back and watched anxiously from a distance as I unwrapped it.

'This is very exciting Emily,' I said. 'Like a birthday.'

She attempted a smile but as always with Emily, at the last moment the corners of her mouth turned down and it became a grimace.

It was a small picture; approximately ten inches by six, set into a larger, bevelled card mount; a landscape in which a wooded escarpment rose majestically out of a lush valley. In style it was reminiscent of a Turner seascape; an impression heightened by the storm clouds the artist had painted which seemed to break like waves on the ridge. There was a dark, brooding quality about the scene that was almost gothic in its intensity. An atmosphere at once magical, and yet strangely disturbing for reasons I'm still unable to explain.

Emily was... is, suffering from multiple personality disorder. In the past, she would have been diagnosed as schizophrenic. Even now, her condition is not recognised as such by many in my profession. Her given name, the one on her birth certificate, identifies her as a thirty-four year old mother of two; a former nurse, married to a computer programmer. And, most of the time, that is who she is. But there are other times, and I've witnessed them myself, when, without warning, her voice will take on the squeaky tones of an eight year old; an obnoxious little girl called Tilly who is strident and argumentative – quite the opposite of Emily's own personality – that is to say, her dominant persona. And it's not just her voice that changes. Emily's whole being seems to shrink in size. Her mouth puckers up defiantly; her shoulders are drawn in and her hands, which normally rest in her lap, gesticulate, point and scratch to emphasise the outpourings of her vicious tongue. Only the eyes seem to grow larger; an effect produced by the dilation of her pupils when Emily is in this transformed state.

The child Tilly has no respect for adults and claims to have brought herself up, after being orphaned at an early age. I've had great difficulty in controlling this alter ego of Emily's and had my face raked by her fingernails on more than one occasion whilst trying to subdue her. These episodes when Emily becomes Tilly can last anything from a few minutes to an hour at a time and come on without warning, causing great distress to her family. Emily herself, has only the vaguest recollection of what she, in the guise of Tilly, has said or done.

'It's a beautiful picture,' I said, holding it out for her to take. 'Thank you for sharing it with me.' I took a step towards her but Emily shrank back from my outstretched hand. 'Emily… what is it? What's the matter?'

'I don't want it,' she said, wild-eyed. 'Please, I want you to have it.' A lock of hair had fallen across her face and she caught it up in her fingers and began twisting it round them. The distraught woman was backed up against the drugs cabinet and I withdrew my hand, increasing the space between us.

'It's very kind of you Emily but I couldn't possibly accept,' I said and taking the picture over to the window, examined it more closely. It wasn't as I had first thought a watercolour, but a print of some kind. I'm no expert in these things, but to my untrained eye it looked like a hand-coloured engraving – a mezzotint perhaps, and the foxing on the yellowed paper suggested great age. 'It looks old,' I said. 'It might be valuable.'

'It is old. Very old,' she confirmed in a tremulous voice.

Emily's reaction to the picture was hard to understand. There was a strangely haunting quality about it, I admit, but nothing I could see that would provoke this irrational fear. What was it about the picture that she found so disturbing? I looked at it again and suddenly realised I was staring at a place that I knew.

'It's Wenlock Edge, isn't it?' I said. 'I used to go

riding there. It's years ago now. I'd almost forgotten. It's a beautiful place.'

'It's a bad place,' said Emily in a voice I hadn't heard before. A voice that wasn't her own; heavily accented and with a distinct Welsh lilt to it. A new personality? Someone she had kept hidden from me all these months; a persona whose appearance had been triggered by the painting perhaps?

'You know the place - it means something to you?' I asked. She didn't answer, so I repeated the question.

'A bad place,' she repeated and crossed herself. She was staring past me as though addressing somebody else. I turned, half expecting to find someone else in the room, but we were quite alone.

'What is your name?' I asked, trying a new tack.

'Griffin, sir, Jane Griffin,' she answered proudly.

'And the year?'

'Why sir, the year of our Lord, sixteen fifty-one,' she replied, evidently surprised by such an obvious question.

1651... history had been one of my favourite subjects at school, so that date had a significance for me. The battle of Worcester had taken place in that year. It was probable then that we were in England at the tail end of The Civil War. But who was Jane Griffin and what was her connection with Wenlock Edge?

'And I am?' I asked in an authoritative voice.

'Why sir, if you don't know...'

'Just answer the question,' I said sternly.

I could see the fear in her eyes now. She was hiding something from me. 'Captain Thomas Aston is the name you gave me sir,' she said curtly.

So, I was a captain, but in whose army? Was I a

roundhead or a cavalier? For Parliament, or the King? The royalists had been defeated at the Battle of Worcester and the future King Charles the Second had fled the field with the roundheads in hot pursuit. Eager for his capture, the Parliamentary forces had scoured the countryside for weeks afterwards looking for him. It was a safe bet then that I was one of Cromwell's Ironsides hunting a fugitive royalist.

'Where is he madam?' I asked, assuming the clipped tones of the military man.

'Who, sir?'

'I think you know who. Pray don't waste my time.'

'I've told you sir – my husband's not here.'

The scene put me in mind of the famous Victorian painting, 'And when did you last see your father?' a romantic depiction of the interrogation in 1642 of Bulstrode Whitelock's children. Following some innate instinct I said, 'Bring in the child.'

The Griffin woman became very agitated at this and began to wail in a pitiful manner.

'No sir. Please don't, I beg of you. She can't tell you anything.'

'I'll be the judge of that madam,' I said, in a voice that surprised me with its roughness and lack of compassion. Something I hadn't experienced before in all my years in practice was at work here. It was as if I'd been taken over by this Captain of Cromwell's troopers and, try as I might, I was unable to drag myself back into the twentieth century. For the moment at least, it was 1651 and I was determined to lay my hands on Sir Ralph Griffin. That too was curious – for how did I know his full name and title? The woman hadn't mentioned it. A scream from Jane Griffin brought these deliberations to an abrupt end.

'Tilly!'

Tilly? The child's name was Tilly? A coincidence, or were all Emily's personalities connected in some way? What strange force was at work here?

'Come here child,' I said, and then to some unseen trooper, 'Bring a bible. Quickly man! Now child,' I continued, 'Do you know what it means to swear on the Holy Book?

'Tilly… NO! If you love your father, say nothing.'

'Be still madam or I will have you removed. Well child?'

'Yes, sir.'

'And you know what happens to those who lie on their oath?'

Emily's eyes grew larger. 'Prithee sir, I do,' she said in the voice I recognised as Tilly's. 'Their souls burn in hell.'

'The child does you credit, my Lady. She will answer true, I'm sure. Now Tilly, where is your father?'

She hesitated and in the silence that followed a voice cried, 'He's making a run for it Captain!' I don't know where the voice came from – Emily, I suppose but I didn't see her lips move.

And suddenly, I could see and hear it all; the man running across the darkened fields; the soldiers in pursuit, moonlight glinting on their breastplates and helmets; the clink of sword in scabbard as they ran. Without thinking, I leapt to my feet and called for my horse. The Griffin woman was on her knees pleading for her husband's life. The child Tilly was crying. I pushed past them both and ran out of the house. In the courtyard, a trooper held a bay mare. Snatching the reins out of his hands, I swung up into the saddle and, with the trooper, the Griffin woman and the child Tilly at my heels, rode off after my quarry.

Most of the harvest had been gathered in and the fields were stubbled and uneven. The fugitive had a head start and was making for a wooded escarpment known as Wenlock Edge that bordered Sir Ralph's lands. Once in those woods we would lose him in the dark. I dug my spurs into the mare's flanks and soon began to overtake the tired troopers. One of them stopped running and raised his musket. I swerved towards him and knocked his weapon up with my sword. 'Fool, I want him alive!' I shouted over the noise of the discharged weapon and, with a shout of encouragement to the rest of the men, rode on.

The moon was higher now and cast an eerie glow over the woods and stubbled fields. A stream marking the boundary of Sir Ralph's estate flowed like quicksilver in its reflection. I leaned into my mount's glossy neck and we soared above the slow-moving stream, silvery droplets falling back into the water. It had been an unusually wet harvest and the brook was deeper and wider than first appeared. We landed heavily, short of the bank, the horse's hindquarters sending up an ice-cold spray that soaked my leather tunic through to my shift. It clung to my back like a second skin and almost immediately I began to shiver like a man with the ague.

The far bank was steeper than that on the other side and deep in mud, so that my mount had some difficulty in climbing out of the freezing water. When we finally topped the rise, we were both caked in mud. I let the tired animal rest for a moment, steam rising from her foam-flecked sides, despite the cold. Before me, the trees on Wenlock Edge cast long shadows across the intervening pastureland, but I spotted our quarry as he ran through a shaft of moonlight, a hundred yards to my left and close to the treeline.

I glanced back the way I had come. The troopers were not far behind me now; I could make out the ruddy face and puffing cheeks of the leading man and, a short way behind, Lady Griffin and her daughter Tilly. Though they were close, I decided to press on alone, rather than wait for them to catch up; try to cut Sir Ralph off before he could reach the shelter of the trees.

The pasture was firmer going and I leaned into my mare's neck once more and spurred her into a gallop. The animal had her second wind now and we cut a broad swathe through the tall grass in the milky moonlight.

When I raised my head again, I could see Sir Ralph silhouetted between two trees, his laboured breathing white and puffy on the cold air. I gave my mount a slap with the flat of my sword and we raced across the remaining open ground, charging into the trees close to the Cavalier's heels. The overhanging branches whipped at my face, clawed at my tunic and hands. I slashed at them with my sword but progress was slow, and Sir Ralph had the advantage of me in this tangle of snares. I slipped from the saddle and, looping the reins over the nearest bough, continued the hunt on foot.

It was much darker in amongst the trees, for although the moon's light filtered down through the branches, it created sinister shapes and shadows that played tricks on the mind and eye. As I had feared, the wooded area provided ample cover for a man wishing to hide from pursuers and in that moment, I thought my quarry had eluded me. Suddenly, the silence was broken by an owl hoot. It was so close that it startled me. There was a crashing of branches and flapping of wings as the bird came cannoning out of some beeches not fifty paces away, and flew straight at me. I raised my arm to protect my face and, when I lowered it again, it was to see Sir Ralph emerge from behind the same tree-trunk.

In a voice hoarse from my exertions, I called upon him to surrender. His reply was a musket ball that buried itself in the bark of a tree, just inches from my head. With a shout of defiance, he turned and began running again. Tired though I was, there was nothing for it but to run on after him and see the game out. Despite my leaden limbs, I was spurred on by the arrival of the rest of the troop. I could clearly hear them now, cursing and fighting their way through the undergrowth behind me.

The trees began to thin, the forest opening out into a small clearing. Ahead, I could see a rocky crag and I realised we had our man trapped. I shouted to the troopers behind me to fan out in a circle. Sir Ralph had reached the edge of the escarpment. There was no way out now but to go down.

Sir Ralph had stopped running. He, too, had realised that the game was up. I surmised his plan had been to hide out in the forest and slip away in the darkness, but he'd been spotted and forced to make a run for it. Drawing his sword, the Cavalier brandished it above his head; the tempered steel blade gleaming wickedly in the silvery light, for the clearing was brilliantly lit by the full moon and I could clearly see the grim determination on our adversary's face – he was going to make a fight of it.

Leaping onto the crag, he took up a crouching stance, weaving the sword blade from side to side, covering the advancing men. We gathered round him in a half-circle, panting like a pack of fox-hounds.

'Put up your sword man,' I entreated him. 'We have no wish to harm you.'

'God save the King,' he shouted defiantly and lunged at the nearest trooper, laying open his arm.

We were about to rush him and take him by the sheer weight of numbers when, with an anguished cry, his wife burst through the circling men. 'For God's sake husband, lay down your sword,' she urged and, grabbing hold of her husband's arm, she pulled herself up onto the crag. For a moment, they clung together in a lover's embrace until the Cavalier's feet, sliding from under him, he lost his footing on the moss covered rock. With a cry of terror, which was echoed by their horrified daughter, the pair went tumbling over the edge.

*

I'm still treating Emily and, since that incident, several other members of the Griffin family have manifested themselves. However, the child Tilly remains at the centre of the problem. I'm convinced that if she can be reconciled with her parents' death as it were, then Emily would be left in peace.

As for the picture, it hung on the wall in my consulting room for a time, though I have since locked it away in one of the clinic's safes. Despite this precaution, I'm still troubled by a recurring dream. In it, I am riding on Wenlock Edge in the moonlight, pursuing a man with a face remarkably like my own. I corner him but, instead of surrendering, he throws up his arms and leaps from the crag into the blackness below.

Stranger still, I find myself talking very knowledgably about the English Civil War in a voice that's not quite my own... not-quite-my-own.

Also by Chris Niblock

BACK DATED

Available in paperback and
as an eBook

1: LOVES LABOURS LOST

Sometimes, it just takes one small disturbance in the calm surface of the everyday; just one thing out of place, to tell the whole story. Breathless after a climb up three flights of narrow stairs, I paused on the landing to catch my breath and find my keys. Even in the dim lighting provided by my rapacious landlord, I could see that the front door to my flat was slightly ajar and I knew immediately that this wasn't an oversight on my part. Closer to, I saw the splintered wood and the well-being engendered by a romantic weekend in Oxford evaporated.

'Don't move anything,' I was told when I reported the break-in to my local outpost of The Met, 'We'll send someone round in the morning.' I barricaded myself in for the night as best as I could, jamming a chair under the door knob, and went to bed. I slept fitfully, alert to every creak and groan of my flat's floorboards and aged plumbing.

The desk sergeant hadn't given me a time and the following day, with breakfast fast becoming a distant memory, I decided to ignore the carnage wrought by my uninvited visitors and try to get some work done. It wasn't easy.

Every room in my one bedroom flat, or 'loft apartment' as the estate agent had rather grandly described it, looked like it had been hit by a mini tornado. In the lounge the entire contents of a large bookcase had been thrown out onto the floor. Spines broken, dust covers ripped off, the precious volumes lay there like a flock of birds with broken wings. Scattered amongst the massacred volumes were first editions of all eight sci-fi novels I'd so far published. The ninth, and the last of a trilogy, was the manuscript I was desperately trying to occupy my mind with.

I took a sip of coffee and grimaced. It was stone cold. I put the mug down and stared at the blank screen in front of me. A fresh chapter full of infinite possibilities stretched out before me. I flexed my fingers and typed chapter twelve in 14pt bold caps, then sat there staring at those two words.

Those thirteen letters.

Those three syllables.

Now what? Suddenly those infinite possibilities seemed all too finite.

Perhaps a fresh shot of caffeine might provide the stimulus required, to propel me and my characters through the next chapter. Pushing back my chair, I stood up and came face to face once more with the reason for my lack of concentration.

I took my coffee mug to the kitchen; a scene of further mindless vandalism: drawers pulled out, cutlery scattered, cupboards emptied, and crockery smashed. I filled the kettle and set it to boil. I'd left the radio playing and on *Woman's Hour* they were having the usual discussion about a man's usefulness, in this brave new world of women's lib. One of the speakers was talking – I thought rather too gleefully – about the *low sperm count* produced by the average male these days. According to this woman, men would soon become redundant as, in the not too distant future, it would be possible to create babies using methods that wouldn't involve sperm. It was a depressing thought, and not one calculated to cheer up this hapless male who was already having a bad day.

I stirred two spoonfuls of demerara sugar into my coffee and returned to the lounge. As I entered the room, a stocky man in a brown leather jacket broke off from examining my new stereo. He had a shaven head, the beginnings of a serious beer gut and the hard-eyed stare of a night club bouncer.

'What are you doing?' I demanded.

'Mister Flaxman?'

'Who wants to know?'

The man put a hand inside his jacket and my alarm increased. Had the burglar returned, this time with a gun?

'D.C. Wells, Garrison Lane Police station,' he replied, producing his warrant card.

I peered at it. I hadn't seen one before, but it looked genuine enough. 'Sorry, for a moment there I thought you were one of the burglars,' I explained. 'Come back for the stereo. Feeling a bit paranoid this morning, I'm afraid.'

'Understandable in the circumstances. Nice stereo. Bang & Olufsen isn't it?'

'Yes. It was a birthday present from my girlfriend.' Why did I sound so defensive?

'Expensive present. She must think a lot of you, that lady of yours.'

I felt my face reddening. It was a mistake to have described Frankie as my girlfriend. Although she was a good five years younger than my thirty-nine, neither of us was in the first flush of youth. The word sounded faintly ridiculous on my lips.

'Yes, she's very generous when it comes to presents,' I said primly. 'Anyway, as you can see, I've been burgled,' I added after an awkward pause.

D.C. Wells looked about him as if he'd only just noticed the mess made by my uninvited visitors. 'So I see.'

'Well, there you have it,' I said, indicating the battered remains of my library with a sweep of a hand. 'My whole life laid out before you. Not necessarily in the right order of course.'

D.C. Wells crouched down and looked them over.

'That's a lot of books.'

'It's a lot of years,' I told him.

Wells pulled one of the volumes out of the pile. 'This one's got your name on it,' he said. He made it sound like an accusation. '*Slave Colony by Ray Flaxman*,' he read. '*The first of the Halgaar Chronicles...*' He got to his feet. '*The Halgaar Chronicles*. What's that then?'

'It's a trilogy I'm writing,' I said.

Wells turned to the back cover. 'Oh, science fiction,' he said scornfully and held it out at arms length as if it was contaminated, or maybe he was just short-sighted.

I took it from him. The dust-jacket had a jagged tear, and a section of the inside pages had been doubled over and badly creased when the book had hit the floor. 'Your colleague at the station told me not to touch anything,' I said pointedly.

'Don't worry Mister Flaxman. I won't have to arrest myself if forensics find my prints in your flat, or you either, should yours turn up here somewhere.' He laughed, a dry, rasping sound. A smoker.

Great. I call for a detective and they send me *The Laughing Policeman*. Suddenly, I could no longer contain the anger that had been building up inside me all morning. These books of mine were like children to me; I'd given birth to them. Nurtured them. Sent them out into the world.

'Instead of standing there making stupid jokes,' I said. 'Why don't you get out there and find the mindless thugs responsible for this... this violation!'

Wells' only reaction was to raise his right eyebrow a fraction. 'With all due respect Mister Flaxman, just where do you suggest I start? Because unless you know their names and addresses, this is where the search for your *mindless thugs* begins.'

Chastened, I turned the battered volume over in my hands. 'They were in mint condition, you see. First editions of all my novels. A lifetime's work...' I controlled myself with an effort; I didn't want to lose it in front of Wells. I doubted if he would understand. 'I'm sorry... bit of a shock coming home to a mess like this.'

'I know sir,' he said and for the first time sounded sympathetic. He took out a small, black note book. 'When was that Mister Flaxman?'

'Uh... late last night. Frankie and I spent the weekend in Oxford...'

'Frankie?'

'My fiancée, Francesca Verde.'

Wells looked puzzled 'You have a fiancée and a girlfriend?'

'No, no. Frankie is my girlfriend. I mean, she's both.' He wrote that down. 'Is she a writer too?'

'No, she's a TV producer. She had an early start this morning, so I dropped her off at her place in Hackney, got back here around midnight.'

More scribbling in the notebook. 'Was the flat left unoccupied for the entire weekend ?'

'Yes. We left London just after lunch on Friday afternoon. Thought we'd beat the rush. We didn't of course. The M25 was more like a car-park than a motorway.'

'So, the thieves had all the time they needed.'

'Sorry, I don't understand. Time for what exactly?'

'You've got some nice things here Mister Flaxman. Wide screen TV, DVD player... that newish laptop there.' He pointed to my apple notebook. 'Not to mention the Bang & Olufsen. All portable, readily saleable in any number of dodgy pubs not a million miles from here and yet,' he paused for effect. 'The thieves left them behind. Curious, don't you think?'

D.C. Wells, I was beginning to realise, was far more canny than he looked. 'Perhaps they were disturbed,' I suggested.

'Maybe.' He took a few strides towards the bookcase, each step accompanied by the sound of crunching glass.

He lifted a foot and examined the sole of his shoe. 'Where's this broken glass from?'

'This picture frame.' I picked up the empty 10 x 8 silver frame from my desk and showed it to him. As he took it from me, the few remaining slivers of glass slid out and joined the rest on the floor. 'It used to contain a photo of my fiancée. The thieves appear to have taken it.'

'Odd...' he said and handed it back to me. His eyes, hard as flint, bored into mine as if trying to read something written on the wall behind my head.

As Wells continued to stare at me and I tried to come up with a convincing reason, why a complete stranger would prefer a portrait of my fiancée to a Bang & Olufsen, the phone rang. 'Excuse me,' I said. 'I'd better answer that. Probably Frankie.' Wells nodded and I picked up the phone.

'Hello.' No response. 'Hello?' I repeated. Still nothing. 'Anybody there?' This time I thought I heard someone breathing on the other end of the line. 'Look, I know you're there. I can hear you breathing, dammit. What's the point of phoning me if you never say anything?' I disconnected and slammed the phone down hard on the desk.

Wells gave me another of his hard-eyed stares. 'You look worried Mister Flaxman. Anything I can help you with?'

'No, nothing. Wrong number that's all.'

Another quizzical raising of an eyebrow. 'I don't think you're being completely honest with me Mister Flaxman.'

'What do you mean?'

'I mean none of this adds up. The thieves had all weekend. They could have walked off with everything you own, yet all they take is a photo of your fiancée. They trash your books, but leave the Bang & Olufsen. And now, you're taking calls from a heavy breather. Sounds like woman trouble to me. So, if there's something you'd like to get off your chest, now would be a good time to do it.'

2: A FAIR COP

Humiliation waited just around the corner for me and desperate to avoid it, I attempted one last defensive bluster. 'Good God, anyone would think I was the criminal here.' I protested.

'I think you'll find withholding evidence and wasting police time *are* both criminal offences sir,' said Wells smugly.

Unable to come up with anything else, I had no choice but to throw myself upon the detective's mercy. We were both men after all, members of the same endangered species. He would understand surely?

'She calls herself Serena.'

'The girl on the phone?'

'No, she never says anything.'

Wells stopped scribbling. He looked puzzled. 'There's another girl?'

'No, no. At least, I don't think so. I'm assuming they *are* one and the same person.'

The detective sighed. 'You're not making much sense, sir. Perhaps if you started at the beginning...' Well, at least I'd wiped that smug look off his face.

'Sorry. It's a bit complicated.' I said. 'And well, you know, somewhat delicate.'

'Yes, I imagine it is sir.' Wells cast an envious glance at the mug of coffee I was nursing, which had now grown as cold as its predecessor.

'Look, why don't I make us both a fresh cup of coffee. While the kettle's boiling, I can collect my thoughts and I'll try to explain what's been going on.'

Wells followed me into the kitchen and stood in the doorway. Perhaps he suspected my offer to make coffee was simply a ploy and that I planned to escape from its third floor window, using a rope I had concealed under the sink. I set the kettle to boil and stared moodily out over the rooftops of Herne Hill towards the leafy greenness of Brockwell Park. I felt trapped, and not just by the physical bulk of D.C. Wells. If Frankie should get wind of what I was about to tell him, I would need a 24hr police presence, to protect me from my fiancée's jealous rage.

Two years or so before we got together, Frankie went through a high profile divorce after her actor husband's affairs with several of his leading ladies was splashed all over the front pages of the tabloids. This very public humiliation had left her bitter and, as I found out to my cost, unable to trust the men in her life.

I first became aware of this at a dinner party we were invited to just a couple of weeks into our relationship. The hostess insisted on splitting couples up and seating them next to a complete stranger. Boy, girl, boy, girl, around the table. I found myself sat between a plump lady vicar, with a good deal of facial hair, and an ageing blonde bombshell, who'd had a small part in an early series of Doctor Who.

I'm an atheist – who was I going to talk to?

I spent the entire evening with the blonde in a lively discussion of the string of actors who had played the time-travelling Doctor, blissfully unaware of the black looks I was getting from Francesca and her bearded table companion. As I later discovered, this gentleman was the blonde woman's husband. This one incident sowed the seeds of Francesca's unwillingness to trust me where women are concerned, and plagues our relationship to the present day. We had a massive row on the way home, after which she refused to speak to me for several days.

'Kettle's boiled sir.'

'What? Oh, right.' I tore my thoughts back from the past, and rinsing a couple of unbroken mugs under the tap, spooned coffee into each of them. I turned to Wells.

'Do you take milk and sugar?'

'Just sugar. Two please.'

He was polite if nothing else. I left mine black too and carried the coffees over to the small kitchen table that stood in a narrow alcove, bordered by a cupboard which contained the central heating boiler and the hot water tank. There was space for just two chairs, one at either end of the oblong melamine-topped table. The detective joined me and we sat facing each other. I counted to ten then began.

'Look, Frankie doesn't have to know about this, does she?' I searched Wells' face for some sign of pity or compassion but found none. 'Only, she and I have been going through a bit of a rough patch lately. The weekend in Oxford was supposed to smooth things over. If she so much as thinks I've been messing around with another woman, let alone a young girl, there'll be hell to pay.'

In fact, the weekend had gone surprisingly well. The cottage Frankie had rented was delightfully rustic and boasted exposed beams, climbing roses and a thatched roof. As we walked up the cobbled pathway, I half expected Anne Hathaway to step out and greet us. We woke the following morning to sunlight dappling the walls of our room and made love for the first time in weeks. That first morning set the mood for the rest of the weekend. It was idyllic, like starring in our very own romcom movie. Best of all, Frankie didn't once nag me to name a date for our wedding, the main reason for the discontent between us in recent months.

When the time came to leave, neither of us had wanted to lock up and return to our everyday lives in twenty-first century London. As I put our bags in the car, I took a last glance at our thatched *love nest* and wished it could always be this way for Frankie and me. We drove home through the darkening countryside, Miles Davis playing *So What* on the car stereo. Cool and blue, the music matched our mood perfectly.

Wells eyed me coldly. I began to feel I'd been over-optimistic in assuming an unspoken camaraderie existed between men, where problems with women were concerned. 'I can't promise to leave the girl out of it at this stage. That would depend on whether she was involved in the break-in or not.'

Accompanied by the occasional burp of water gurgling in the tank behind me, I thought this over. If it was up to me, I'd rather pay for the damage done to my flat myself than have this little titbit of mine pop up in *The News of the World*. 'O.K., between you and me then.' I said. 'I've been getting letters as well as the phone calls.'

'Letters. What sort of letters?'

'Love letters of course!' I snapped.

Wells shot me a warning look. 'From this Serena? You kept them?'

'Yes. It was stupid, I know.'

'Not as stupid as writing to *her* – you didn't, did you?'

'No, of course not. Couldn't, even if I'd wanted to. I don't have her address.'

'Pity. About the address, I mean. Well, can I see them?'

I held my head in my hands. 'I'm afraid not. The thieves took them.'

Wells leaned forward, the glimmer of a smile playing about his thin lips. 'At last. Now we're getting somewhere. He dipped a hand into a jacket pocket.

'Mind if I smoke?'

'Be my guest,' I said. 'I'll just open the window.' I got up and leaned over the sink. The window frame was old and tended to stick, but after a brief struggle I managed to open it six inches or so. 'Why do you think they took the letters... and the photo, what's that about?' I asked.

Wells held an unlit cigarette between his lips. It bobbed up and down as he spoke. 'Well, if you're lucky, she just wanted her letters back and the photo's still here somewhere.'

'And if not?'

Wells fired up a red *zippo* lighter and lit his cigarette. He took a long drag at it and, leaning back in his chair, exhaled loudly. 'This Serena's sending you a message.

You've really pissed her off and if you don't start being nice to her, she's going to spill the beans to your fiancée. The photo is proof that she knows you.'

I hadn't considered that possibility. It came as something of a shock. 'Blackmail, you mean? Oh, I don't think she's capable of that.'

Wells snorted. 'Why not? She's capable of trashing your flat, or at least getting someone to do it for her.' He took another drag and sent a blue ring of smoke spiralling towards me. 'Hell hath no fury and all that.'

'My God. What am I going to do?' I said.

'You could always deny it.' said Wells. 'She has nothing in writing from you, and the photo was stolen during a break-in. 'What was in these letters anyway?'

I paused for a moment. Tried to picture the words on the page, the backward slope of the flowery script; a left-hander? A young woman's hand anyway.

'Oh, just schoolgirl stuff really. Did I miss her? Did I still love her? You know the kind of thing.' I found myself blushing as I repeated these fragments. If Wells noticed my discomfort, he mercifully refrained from commenting on it.

The detective thoughtfully sipped his coffee whilst he considered this information. 'How long ago was it that you and her...?'

'There was no *me* and her!' I said, slamming my mug down on the table so hard that globules of coffee shot over the rim and splashed my shirt sleeve. 'I've no idea who the girl is, or what she's talking about. She's got me mixed up with some other guy, or else she's got a screw loose. I don't know which. Do you have any escaped loonies on your books at the moment?'

'That description covers a fair percentage of the people I meet during the course of my work Mister Flaxman.'

I may be over-sensitive, but I couldn't help thinking that he included me in that list.

'Of course.' continued Wells. 'This deranged girl could just be a fan of yours...'

I didn't like the implication that only the deranged were likely to read my books, but I couldn't discount the possibility that the stalker was one of my readers. It would explain why someone I'd never met might write to me.

'Well yes, I do have fans who take my work a bit too seriously. A lot of sci-fi writers have their 'Trekkies' so to speak.' I admitted.

'Trekkies?'

'You know... *To boldly go*? People who like to dress up as Captain Kirk and Mister Spock?' The original TV series was long before his time and mine I know, but what planet had Wells been living on, not to have heard of possibly the most influential Sci-fi series of all time. 'Star Trek.' I informed him, barely disguising my incredulity at his ignorance. 'It was a 'must watch' TV series in the sixties that inspired a lot of the guys who worked for NASA. It's still on TV in one form or another: Star Trek Voyager, Star Trek: The Next Generation... Deep Space Nine and there's been half a dozen feature films. You've really never heard of it?'

'No... I prefer Sky Sport myself. Do your fans dress up then?'

I pictured this for a moment. As a marketing tool it had a certain appeal. 'Not as far as I know.' I said. This admission made me feel a bit of a failure. My characters, as depicted on the covers of my novels, weren't lacking in sex appeal, so why didn't my fans feel the urge to dress like them? Perhaps it was the skimpiness of the costumes, I decided; they were hardly suited to the British climate, even in summertime.

'They usually just want to know stuff about the characters that isn't in the books.' I said lamely. 'Like, do they have a favourite colour? What their star signs are? Stuff like that.' Wells looked disappointed. 'Mundane stuff. Nothing that would explain this. Still, perhaps this girl thinks I'm Bors and she's Princess Twala...'

'Who, sir?'

'Never mind, just characters from my novels.'

'Oh, right.' Wells downed the last of his coffee and, crossing to the window, stubbed his cigarette out in the sink. 'Well, there's not much more I can do here. I'll let you have a crime number for your insurance company. As nothing of monetary value has been taken, I doubt if we'll be sending forensics round. Any further developments, give me a ring on this number.' He produced a business card.

'Thanks,' I said, taking it from him. 'Hopefully, I won't need it. If you're right, and the girl's got what she wants, perhaps she'll leave me in peace now.'

Wells gave me a pitying look. 'In my experience,' he said. 'It's a rare woman that's satisfied with what she's got.'

Dolefully, I followed him out into the lounge. At the front door he paused.

'One more thing,' he said, and opening the door wide, he pointed to a large, black smudge in the white paintwork on the other side. 'I'd be careful if I were you sir. Your little princess's friend has got very large feet.'

3: MISS LONELY HEARTS

After the detective had gone, I took one of my shoes and placed it over the footmark on the door's paintwork. I take a size nine and I'm a skinny, five foot ten. The mark on the door was a good five centimetres longer than the sole of my shoe and I estimated Serena's accomplice must be well over six foot. Writing works of fiction requires a vivid imagination. The image mine conjured up of the footprint's owner was a cross between *Quasimodo* and *The Incredible Hulk*. In my mind, I saw this giant place massive hands on the walls either side of him and, bracing himself, burst the door open with one swift kick.

Feeling decidedly uneasy, I quickly shut the door and barricaded myself in again by wedging a chair under the door knob. I dug out the *Yellow Pages* and, with shaking hands, looked up the number of a 24hr locksmith. I rang the mobile number listed and, after some delay, a chirpy voice answered. The man, named appropriately enough Trevor Locket, assured me that he'd have my flat well and truly secured before nightfall.

Feeling only slightly less apprehensive about my personal safety, I then phoned my publisher, told him what had happened and extracted a promise from him that he would do his best to locate and replace the damaged copies of my own titles.

Fired up now, I decided to press on and clear up the mess 'Big Foot' had made of my home. Starting with the books, I stacked them up on the floor in piles according to genre: plays in one pile, thrillers in another and so on, fantasy and science fiction forming the tallest stacks. Then genre by genre I put them back on their appropriate shelves in the bookcase.

The biggest job done, I collected up the scattered ornaments and returned them to their allotted places on mantelpiece and window sill, then set about sorting and filing the paper chase of utility bills and personal documents that littered the floor. Finally, I hoovered up as much as I could of the glass fragments from the smashed picture frame and stood back to admire my handiwork. To the casual observer the room looked more or less as it had on the day I left for Oxford; the broken spines and torn dust jackets of my books the only real sign that anything untoward had occurred.

That just left the bedroom and the kitchen to sort out. I decided to tackle the bedroom first, as there was less to do in there and, if necessary, I could always leave the kitchen until the morning. I'd just finished re-making the bed when a rat-tat-tat on the front door announced the arrival of the locksmith. I removed my improvised barricade and let him in.

Mister Locket was a small, dapper man in his fifties with a shock of salt 'n' pepper hair and an annoyingly cheerful manner.

'ad some uninvited guests, 'ave yer?' he said cheerily. 'Look at this mess,' he added, tutting over the splintered door jamb. 'Just kicked the door in - bloody amachers! I could've opened it in less than thirty seconds with just two sheets of thin plastic and you wouldn't 'ave known I'd been 'ere.'

'I suspect the guy responsible has more brawn than brain.' I said.

'Well, whotja expect,' said the little man. 'Leave school unable to bloody read or write 'alf of 'em.'

Big Foot had made it abundantly clear that he didn't have much interest in reading, but I thought it unlikely that illiteracy had reached anything like that level amongst the general population; although it would go some way to explaining why my royalty cheques never quite matched my expectations.

'Right,' I said non-committally.

'Want me to replace the existing lock, or fit summink that'll break the toes orff the next little toe-rag ooh tries to kick the door in?' Trevor enquired, as he flipped open the lid of his toolbox.

'This particular toe-rag was far from little,' I said. 'If the size of the footprint he left on my door is anything to go by, but I take your point. How much would this 'toe-breaker' lock thing cost me?'

'Well nah, let me see,' he said, pulling a printed price list from his overalls.

The price quoted, after some protracted calculations, was astronomical, but peace of mind and self preservation demanded that I have it. How ironic, I thought, that a 'toe-breaker' should cost me an arm and a leg.

'O.K., go for it,' I said, after some quick mental calculations of my own.

Whilst Trevor went back to his van to fetch this apparently gold-plated, diamond-encrusted superlock, I made him a mug of tea: 'milk and three sugars ta,' then buckled down to sorting out the kitchen.

An hour later and several hundred pounds the poorer, my front door was secured against all assailants bar those armed with plastic explosives, and the kitchen more or less restored to its former faded glory. I'd have to go out and replace the broken crockery, but that could wait until tomorrow, I thought.

I put in a call to Frankie's mobile, but it went straight to voicemail. I wasn't surprised; I knew she was working late on a big crime drama series that involved a night shoot. There was little point in leaving a message, and Monday wasn't an evening that we normally spent together anyway.

I put a *Crowded House* album on the stereo and, with the kitchen door open, put an omelette together using some left over chicken and a slightly shrivelled green pepper to the strains of *Don't Dream it's Over*. By the time I slipped my dinner plate into the washing up bowl, the lads from the Antipodes were singing *Everything is Good for You*.

I retired to the living room and poured myself a large glass of Chilean Merlot from a screw-top bottle. Some people are sniffy about them and insist on cork stoppers, but I prefer them myself. According to the label, I was about to enjoy a full-bodied red with a hint of blackcurrant, mulberries and plum. I took a mouthful and swilled it around my tongue. The wine tasted... well, like Merlot, then what did I know? It was red. It cost £3.99 a bottle and it was 12.5% alcohol by volume. There were at least another three large glassfuls left in the bottle and after the day I'd just had, that was all I required of it. I was drinking to forget: to forget the desecration of my flat and belongings, the small fortune I'd paid the locksmith for his services and the disturbing fact that, somewhere out in the gathering darkness, was a deluded girl who claimed to be my lover and her anthropoid accomplice.

It was comforting, even reassuring therefore, to reawaken my 'snoozing' laptop and return to that other world of mine; where gravity was one third of earth's and where I could become a muscular giant of a man myself in the shape of Bors, hero of *The Halgaar Chronicles*.

As the screen came to life, those familiar words set in 14pt bold caps returned to taunt me. I took a large sip of Merlot and after a moment's contemplation, the warm fruity taste of the wine still on my tongue, words began to form in my mind and flowed through my fingers onto the screen.

Exhaustion had finally forced sleep upon them. They lay in each other's arms on a rocky outcrop, high above a deep canyon. Bors didn't know how long they had been asleep, but when Princess Twala stirred, he was instantly awake, alert to each new sound and scent, his powerful body coiled like a big cat, ready to spring into action. Slipping off his cloak and draping it over the sleeping girl beside him, Bors inched his way toward the edge of the precipice.

As Halgaar's twin moons rose above the horizon, Bors sensed a thousand eyes peering from the shadows along the tree-line. They were close now, he could feel it; almost smell their foetid breath on the wind blowing through the canyon. Soon, they would break cover and come after the girl. Bors turned, and started back down the rocky outcrop, skinning his knees on its needle-sharp ridges...

The phone must have rung several times before it registered with me. It was only after I'd typed the same sentence twice, that I became aware of what had broken my concentration. I snatched up the phone, said 'Hello.' There was no response from the other end of the line, just the sound of someone breathing. It was that damned girl again!

'Look here, I've had just about enough of this nonsense.' I shouted into the mouthpiece. 'So why don't you just go...'

'Ray?' queried an all too familiar voice. Is that you? It's me, Frankie.'

Like a runaway train hitting the buffers, my angry tirade was brought to an abrupt halt. Horrified, I tried to crawl out of the wreckage my hasty outburst had wrought.

'Frankie? Darling, I'm so sorry. I thought you were somebody else.'

'Obviously,' came the tart reply. 'Anyone I know?'

'What?' I burbled, my brain racing to catch up with my runaway tongue. 'Oh... no, a wrong number, that's all.'

'Are you always that rude to people who ring you by mistake?'

'No, of course not, but she's rung me several times today already.'

'She?'

I should have chosen my words more carefully. A second train was approaching fast and about to run into the back of the first.

'He, she... whoever. They never actually say anything, just breathe at me.'

'But you assumed it was a woman. Why is that, I wonder?'

'I could have chosen either sex. There are only two to choose from, you know.'

'But still you chose to use she...'

'Frankie, please. Don't do this. We've just spent a wonderful weekend together. I came home feeling all warm and fuzzy round the edges to find my flat had been vandalised.' I was choosing my words carefully now.

'I've spent all day dealing with the police, with locksmiths and heavy breathers; not to mention putting my flat back in order. This is the first chance I've had all day to sit down and do some serious writing.' I could feel my jangled nerves getting the better of me. 'You're not the only one working to a deadline you know Frankie. Christ!'

A stunned silence from the other end, then Frankie sounding subdued asked, 'Are you all right? You sound a bit strange.'

Strange! I'd spent most of the day scared shitless. I couldn't tell her that of course, for fear that talk of *Big Foot* might lead to further unintended revelations regarding the sender of those unsolicited and, as of yesterday, missing love letters. 'Strange' just didn't cover how I was feeling right now. I took a long sip of Merlot to steady my nerves before replying.

'I'm O.K.,' I assured her. 'Just feeling a bit got-at, that's all. Though it's hardly surprising in the circumstances.' Wouldn't have thought I needed to point that out, I thought but didn't say so. 'And to cap it all, I'm way behind on this damned book. I really must finish this chapter tonight. So, if you don't mind, can I call you tomorrow?'

'Y-e-s, all right then as long as you're sure you're all right.' She sounded hurt. 'Don't work all night, will you?'

'No, I won't. Bye then. Love you.'

'Bye... love you too.'

She'd barely got the words out before I disconnected; I was that eager to avoid any further probing from her. It brought to mind the old wartime maxim: *careless talk costs lives*. Although in this case, it was likely to be the 'family jewels' that I sacrificed. I put the phone down on its block and returned to my keyboard with hands that were shaking.

'Pull yourself together Flaxman,' I told myself and concentrated on typing one letter after another onto the virtual sheet of blank paper that glowed on my laptop in the darkened room. After a while I got back into the rhythm and managed to add a further five hundred words or so to those I'd already written under the Chapter Fourteen heading. During that time I became Bors, hero and champion of the deposed Princess Twala of Halgaar, who faced extinction at the hands of the Barbarian Hordes which surrounded them.

I literally jumped out of my chair when the doorbell rang, as if the Barbarians were gathered at my gate. For Pete's sake. What now, I wondered? Before I'd had time to get to the door and find out the bell rang again. Of all the people who could be out there, it was unlikely to be

Big Foot, I decided. He was a gatecrasher, not a bell- ringer kind of guy.

'All right, I'm coming,' I shouted. Whoever it was, they were leaning on the doorbell now. 'What's so bloody urgent?' I demanded as I threw open the door. Before I could stop her, she'd pushed her way in, a young blond, dressed as if for a '60's revival night' party, in a short, very short, black and white dress, white knee length boots and a matching shoulder bag.

'Close the door!' she commanded.

I was still staring at her legs. She was showing a good deal of them under that retro dress of hers.

'Close the damned door!' She snapped and, crossing to the window, peeled back the curtain to peer outside. 'I think they may have followed me here.'

I stopped looking at her legs then. This was beginning to look like a scene from an old, black and white Bogart movie.

'They? Who are they?' I said. 'And more to the point, who the devil are you?'

'Ray darling, that's not funny...'

'Whoa... what did you just call me?'

'Ray. That's your name isn't it? Raymond when you're naughty.'

'No. The other thing.'

'What other thing... what are you on about?'

'Darling. You called me darling.'

'Darling? Yes, of course dar-ling.' She opened her arms wide. 'Come here and give me a big hug. I've missed you.'

The penny finally dropped along with my jaw. Afterwards I found it hard to believe I hadn't caught on sooner.

'Oh, no. Oh my God, no. You're her, aren't you? You're little Miss Lonely Hearts!' I bore down on her with murder in my heart. Dropping her arms, the girl backed away, her eyes wide with fear, or disappointment, or perhaps it was both. It was hard to tell. 'You've got some nerve waltzing back in here as sweet as you like, after what you've done.' I grabbed her roughly by the shoulders. 'Have you any idea how much grief your antics have caused me?' A vivid image flashed into my mind of *Big Foot* bracing himself to kick my door in and, behind him, Miss 'butter wouldn't melt in her mouth' egging him on. 'Stay there,' I said and, running back to the door, slammed it shut.

The door secured, I turned my attention to the girl. It was hard not to feel sorry for her; all the life seemed to have gone out of her, and she was slumped against the wall like a rag doll. 'Are you alone or did you bring your friend with you – the one with the big feet?'

'Friend. What Friend?' She said dully, her eyes downcast. 'I don't know what you're talking about. I don't have any friends here.' She looked up and, fixing me with eyes full of sadness, said, 'I only have you.'

'Me? But you don't know me,' I said. 'And I don't know you. These feelings of yours are misplaced – a delusion.'

'What would you know about feelings? The others were right. Men are selfish and brutal.'

'Brutal? That's rich! I'm not the one who goes round trashing people's flats. Anyway, if you hate men so much, I should stay away from them, and that includes me.'

The girl straightened herself to her full height and took several steps towards me. 'I don't hate you. I love you. I was fool enough to believe that you loved me.'

Fool is right, I thought. 'There you go again. Why do you persist with this ridiculous fantasy? We are not in love. We never have been. Look, I don't know how to break this to you, but *The Halgaar Chronicles* are just stories I make up. Me, not *Bors* and you, not *Princess Twala*. O.K. Now please, go home and get a life!'

'Selfish, brutal *and* cruel,' she said slowly and deliberately. 'Whatever made me think you would be the ideal man to father my child.'

I didn't know who to phone first, the police or the men in white coats. It was tragic, such an attractive girl, but madder than a box of frogs.

'Now you want my babies! Well, you'll have to join the queue, I'm afraid. My fiancée got in first and if she has her way, we'll be having at least three little Flaxmans, God help us. I think that's more than enough, don't you?' At least three too many as far as I was concerned, which was partly why I'd been dragging my feet on the marriage thing, but it seemed the more I resisted the more determined Frankie became to have her way, and she was a woman used to getting what she wanted.

Before I could stop her, the girl rushed me and began pounding my chest with her fists.

'Ray, I lost the baby,' she screamed at me. 'I need you to get me pregnant again!'

ABOUT THE AUTHOR

Chris Niblock was born in London but now lives in
Shropshire. *Soul Trader* is his second novel. He is also an
artist and amateur musician and regularly plays guitar and
sings in his local café bar. You can read his blog and view
a selection of Chris's artwork on his website at
www.chrisniblock.com

www.ingramcontent.com/pod-product-compliance
Lightning Source LLC
Chambersburg PA
CBHW070613130626
46556CB00001B/351